The Bea

By

Yvonne Bloor

I would like to dedicate the book to my beautiful daughter and wonderful son in law

Acknowledgment

My dear friend June Shaw for her wonderful photography of Trow Rocks at Sandhaven Beach

Chapter 1

It was a wet and windy day as Jacqueline looked out of her bedroom window in the three bedroomed house, which she shared with her husband Declan and their three children, Emily, Niamh, and Colm. The Gibsons' household was always full of energy. Jacqueline was up early that morning in January 1962, as the rest of the family were sleeping in their beds. Jacqueline was preparing for her usual Sunday visit to church at St Bernadette Roman Catholic Church. The children were not that enthusiastic but did attend church from time to time. Declan didn't really aspire to Sundays being a day of rest, as he was a working miner, a deputy manager, and only knew Sundays as a day of work, at least most Sunday mornings. He had the constitution of an ox and worked hard to provide for his family.

Emily was the oldest child, aged fifteen. She was a shy-natured girl. She sat brushing her long dark hair that would fall to the middle of her back. How she loved her arts and crafts. A fair contrast to her younger sister who was thirteen years old. As Niamh was an extrovert, you could say she was the voice of the family, as Niamh would take every opportunity to read in front of an audience. "Another book, our Niamh! Must you!" Emily would sigh.

They had a younger brother, Colm, ten years old. He was the mischievous one of them all, with his thick set of brown hair. It was always "anything will do" with Colm. He would just brush his hair with his hands and put his cap on, for he loved his Newcastle football team and couldn't wait to go the football matches with this dad and Uncle Dylan. He wouldn't been seen without his favourite black and white cap; he was a typical lad who loved to go out with his friends and explore and wander around the beachy heads along the coastline. Being a good artist, he loved to sketch out the birds by the sea.

The Gibsons were a close family and they shared everything together, even their disagreements, and there were some, but they always seemed to mend everything before bedtime; that was the rule of the house.

The fresh winds were picking up and Jacqueline was late as she rushed off to Mass. She always took a moment to look across to Trow Rocks that stood firmly in the sea. It always reminded her of a beautiful painting, so elegant as the wind lashed out and flirted with the rocks. Jacqueline stood and watched with amazement as the water caressed itself around the magnificent cliffs. Jacqueline would always find the poetic meaning in a beautiful landscape, for South Shields had a multitude of beautiful landmarks, not to mention the great Disappearing Gun mounted with pride, a symbolic creature resonating across the land searing in the distance. Oh, but it was one of those days! The wind was lashing loudly, and the sea was whimpering, and the waves were getting higher… The sea and its romantic effect, after all, is nature at his best. Jacqueline smiled to herself as she entered church and thanked God for the beautiful life she had.

As Mass ended, Jacqueline met up with her dear friends Lydia and Polly at the coffee morning which was a ritual after Mass. They always brought cakes and biscuits for the priest, Fr Donnelly, and other members of the church. The tables were always carefully set out after Mass, each table having its individual tablecloths to demonstrate the owner. The members of the coffee morning were selective, as they were the ones who inherited the coffee morning ritual from many years ago. They took pride in the tables which included homemade biscuits, scones, and every cake you could think of. Joan, Gloria, Lydia and Polly were the selected few to make up their tables. Jacqueline contributed with her skill of cake making which she candidly displayed at the back of the room, which everyone took advantage of. Fr Donnelly always hogged the cake stand…

The conversation around the room began rather intensely, as there was always the same group talking over one another. Jacqueline gazed over to the bun stand, and she smiled and

2

slowly exited the room so as not to be noticed; Jacqueline was not going to be caught up in the intense conversations of who baked the best. "It is time to head home for lunch,", she said to herself as she caught Fr Donnelly's eye and waved her usual signal. Fr Donnelly acknowledged the signal and waved back.

Sunday lunch at the Gibsons' was always a treat for the family because Jacqueline was renowned for the best Yorkshire puddings in the land. They loved it! Also, the pudding, apple crumble and custard, never failed to impress. As the family sat around the roaring coal fire blistering away, the conversations flowed as the Gibsons always talked to one another.

Emily shouted up to show her new crochet pattern. "Do you like it, Mam? I am making this for you."

"Aww, pet, that is so lovely. It will look beautiful on the table."

Emily's creativity with a needle, thread, and knitting needles always amazed her mam, but she was not blessed academically. Jacqueline was so close to her first-born, having had a difficult birth at home.

There was always time for reading, and Niamh once again would grasp the opportunity of reading out loud. As they all sat around the fireside, Niamh began reciting one of her favourite poems, 'Stop all the Clocks', by WH Auden. She came across the book at the local library, as she was always there.

Emily spouted up, "Ooh that's such a sad poem."

Niamh replied, "It is, but it's showing a lot of passion, emotion! The feelings of loss! The author is telling us that we must all stand still and motionless for that moment in time, it's so meaningful as she jumps up! It's the depth of the writer that gets you!"

3

"Alright, our Niamh," their father said as he put his hand on her shoulder. "Let's simmer down with those emotions, shall we."

Niamh gasped and sat down with her book in hand. She loved to explore the characters and plots, and to figure out what the author was trying to say to her.

Jacqueline looked across at Niamh with loving eyes and said, "You are a dreamer of imagination, just like your mam."

Colm looked on pensively. Nothing deterred Colm. He just murmurs. "Cannot understand what you are on about? I am off to call on Tom to play a game of footie…" Tom was his best friend. Declan was lost in his newspaper; after all, it was a Sunday afternoon…

Colm was the only one yet to be confirmed at the Catholic Church, and he was not looking forward to it. He felt it was OK to say your prayers before bed and that should be enough, bless him.

Jacqueline sat Colm down and said, "It's not going to happen straightaway. You will have to go through the process first, as you know. Your teacher would have spoken about it, I am sure."

"She may have," Colm said, "but I probably wasn't listening." Colm slumped back in the chair.

"Your Auntie Aileen is going to be your sponsor for your confirmation. You love your Auntie Aileen."

"OK Mam… No bother…" Colm said as he slumped away to his room…

Jacqueline sent a note to Aileen asking her to come around for tea next Sunday to smooth things over with Colm. Jacqueline was so good at peace-making and turning things around.

4

All was calm and cosy on a Sunday night. The family would gather. Colm came downstairs to join them all, for they were playing a game of Monopoly and there was always drama! Colm loved to wind Niamh up by jumping past his mark on the board.

"It's eight thirty, time for bed," Declan said.

Colm turned to his dad with a disapproving look. "Why can't we stay up like Emily!"

"When you are fifteen, lad, you can and that's that! Those are the rules, and you know they are."

Colm stood up, shrugged his shoulders and went up to bed, shouting at the top of the stairs, "It's not fair!"

Emily was too busy with her crochet to notice the argument. She was making progress with her tablecloth and was getting excited as it was almost finished. It was a masterpiece, so delicate, almost like an oil painting. Emily was the delicate child, always suffering with her asthma. She was feisty with it though and wouldn't give in to it… It was getting better as she was getting older.

Niamh always seem to be protective of Emily even though she was a little bit younger. They would sit cross-legged on the bedside and talk for hours sometimes. They both loved the same music and talked about fashion and new hair styles. They would practise new hair styles on each other and laugh and giggle together.

As Jacqueline sat back in the armchair, she seemed to step back in time to when she was seventeen; a time when she was consumed with how she looked and felt, as that was the time Jacqueline had met Declan, who was eighteen months younger than her. They'd become inseparable. They knew each other inside out. Jacqueline always liked to remind Declan of the night they met at the local dance, for she loved to dance, whilst Declan wasn't that keen. The only reason he went to the dance was because he knew Jacqueline would be there. She had caught his eye at the local post office and he'd overheard Jacqueline talking to someone in the queue about how the local dance was the sensation of the week. Declan couldn't take his eyes off her. From that moment on he had made his mind up to go to the dance. Declan's mates were flabbergasted! Declan Gibson going to a dance was never heard of...

Jacqueline was a petite girl, with her brown hair and big brown eyes and an infectious smile. Declan stood at 5ft 8ins, with his broad shoulders and dark hair. His deep brown eyes couldn't help but notice Jacqueline on the dance floor. His friends said to him, "Well, Dec, you are going to have to dance now mate, if you want to chat her up..." Declan got rid of his cigarette, walked nervously towards Jacqueline, and asked her to dance. In that moment he was dancing on air...

Declan was a young man who worked down the local pit, and Jacqueline was a scholar who was thriving in her studies. They would meet up twice a week, in secret as their parents would not have approved of Declan. It had worked well for some time until Jacqueline's parents tried to put a stop to their meetings. She lay back in the armchair, smiling with joy as she recalled the audacity of Delcan, his passion, his belief that he had found the love of his life and no one would stop that, not even her parents. He would walk miles to meet her, and one night he got the scolding of his life! Mr Gannett, Jacqueline's father, had caught sight of them both. "Get in the house, Jacqueline, this minute!" Jacqueline was too startled to not obey her father.

Declan and Mr Gannett eyed each other up and Declan got his words out fast. "I am in love with your daughter, and I intend to marry her one day!"

"Not in my lifetime, lad. Get yourself off before I give you a good tanning!"

Declan glared at Mr Gannett and took a step back, but wasn't prepared to cause a scene as Declan was not a brawler in the street. Mr Gannett was surprised he walked away, but gave a sigh of relief as he thought to himself, *I think it would have been me who got the tanning.*

It was a long-haul, lengthy romance. The twists and turns, the overriding bickering from each party was never ending, but the love that Delcan and Jacqueline felt was not going to fade, and all parties realised that it was going to happen.

It was a night of reminiscing. Declan and Jacqueline cosied up at the big open fire which was roaring away. "We have come along way, pet, since that night at the dance. Happy?"

"I couldn't be happier, my love. Who wouldn't be? Three gorgeous kids and a not bad husband."

Declan grabbed Jacqueline in a wrestling match. "Not bad, aye?" They laughed and laughed. "Bed, Mrs," as Declan rolled his eyes...

Declan was up and out at 5am for his Monday morning shift... Jacqueline was whimpering with delight at their night together. He kissed her passionately and whispered, "Love you forever."

Jacqueline replied, "Love you more." Their passion, their togetherness was so apparent; their heartbeats beat as one. They knew every inch of each other, every movement, every desire to be completed. They were perfection...

Jacqueline lay in bed, whimpering with pleasure, and often wondered that if Declan hadn't gone to that dance that night, she may have gone out with Ray Marston, a tall blonde lad who worked at the local butchers. He tried in vain to get Jacqueline's attention on numerous occasions, The very thought of it now made her laugh so much. *As if I would choose Ray Marston; he was a polite lad but didn't seem to have much personality. He always talked about train spotting, he was obsessed with it. How happy I am, how blessed I am*, she thought. *Ooh, I best get up before the kids, get the show on the road. It's a busy Monday ahead...*

Chapter 2

It was Monday morning the wind had died down and the sun is shining over a very calm sea, and the golden sand is glistening. Jacqueline was lively with her daily take of chores, "I must get all this rubbish in the bins ready for the bin collection, as she walked to the bottom of the garden opened the gate to take in the sea breeze. The seagulls were singing their song, as they were all flickering and flapping merrily along the beach head towards the rocks. Jacqueline at that moment thought of all the poems she loved, and one came to mine, Shelley and his moon beams.... "The sunlight clasps the earth and moonbeams kissed the sea .... "How she loved the Romantic poets, Keats, being her ultimate favourite, Byron was hard to digest at times with his revolutionary approach to poetry, but she loved his poem, "She walks in Beauty".

Jacqueline had her 5 minutes of solitary embrace with the sea and sand, and the romantic poets... Back to reality.... let's get the morning organised she shouted, "come on kids time you were off to school", Emily and Niamh walked together, they were always together. Emily looked up to Niamh, as she felt that her sister had all the answers and she believed everything Niamh told her. As Emily had her struggles with schoolwork, she could never understand how to make a good sentence or even write a good composition. Niamh always there to help her along whatever the situation.

Colm was laid back and took everything in his stride; he loved drawing, especially seagulls, and paid particular attention to their eyes, he would perch himself between Trow Rocks and study them awhile before putting pencil to paper, he would spend hours on Trow Rocks. If there were seagulls in his life and football Colm was one happy lad.

No one could have foreseen the accident on Trow Rocks that was to occur that very night on the beach.... .... After school had finished, Colm and Tom decided to go down to the Beach. The history lesson that they sat through earlier in class had spurred them on. Mr Beckett the History teacher explored the year 1782 as he introduced the class to the favourite spots where smugglers would land and descend onto the beach, in fact some lived in the caves, poaching, expecting to find treasures and did. Colm and Tom were so attentive in class and Mr Beckett was amazed at the transformation.

As Colm and Tom left school, they had got it into their heads that they might find some hidden treasure in one of the caves. They went high up on to the rocks as there were so many caves on top as well as below. Colm thought the high spots seemed more hidden away as they delved in and out of the rocky steps, Tom was way behind. Colm hollowed, "Come on Tom mate get a shifty on man" As Colm turned the rock slid and crumbled underneath him, he yelled out!! And lost his footing. He was flying… all he could think of was, I can swim! He fell headfirst into the sea…. He was underwater scrabbling…. the waves were pushing him out to sea, he was attempting to do a breaststroke as he was a good swimmer, but it was not working the waves were pushing and pushing until eventually he was pushed against a hard surface, it was a buoy he felt a rope and grabbed onto it, gasping for breath! He was way out! and the mist had started to form, and the winds had picked up, it was dark now at 6pm. Colm was now gasping for breath! He was struggling to stay afloat! as the waves were folding all over him…. And over him… He used his upper body strength to hold on, he was a strapping lad just like his dad.

Tom at this time was frantic, he ran and ran… back to the Gibson's banging on the back door as it was closer to the beach. Jacqueline opened the door, Tom was panting hard, he couldn't get his words out at first, Jacqueline told him to breathe slowly…. until eventually he calmed a little. Jacqueline went straight to Lynda's next door to see if her husband Brian could drive to the pit head and get a message to Declan. Jacqueline was so focused she ran to the coast guard, and he alerted the lifeboat teams; and the lighthouse keeper Jake would keep a close eye on the waters to see if he could spot Colm. The fog had drawn in and it was so hard to see anything out at sea… Declan had arrived at the beach head, he got into one of the boats to go out at sea, Jacqueline wanted him to stay back and let the lifeboat team do their job, Declan wasn't having that, he wanted to be out there. Time was of the essence! It had been three hours since the search began and the lifeboat rescue team radioed in to say, "|Nothing yet, we will keep on with the search". Declan was escorted onto a dinghy towards the Rescue Team. They circled around and around… It was Declan who suggested they go on the south side of the rocks, as he knew Colm would be on the south side, he was sure of that. It was a challenge given the fog, but the lifeboat team knew their course through thick fog.

Colm at this time was holding onto the buoy with his right hand as his left was now numb… Colm began to murmur "Dear God, I know I am not a great Catholic, I do believe in you. I promise I will go to church and enjoy my confirmation if you get me out of the sea and back home, please …. I don't think I can hold on much longer…. I hope you got my message "

The lifeboat team steered to the south side, Colm could hear someone, he was too cold and couldn't get the strength to shout back. He lifted his left arm and tried to wave as best he could. Jake in the lighthouse noticed a movement and got on the radio to alert the lifeboat team, "Looks like some movement at the buoy to left of you ". They got there! They found Colm! He was delirious! Thank you, God! Colm kept saying… and saying… They wrapped him in foil and got him straight to the hospital. Jacqueline was on the beach with her Rosary Beads out and on the 10th Hail Mary as she received the good news… she would always turn to her Rosary as that was her greatest strength. Jacqueline believed everyone had a faith, different cultures, different tongues, but the same outcome she was sure of that.

Colm was to stay in hospital for a few days as he was suffering with severe hyperthermia. The Doctor approached Declan and Jacqueline, "Colm has suffered a bump on his left side, brought about by banging into the buoy it seems, he is otherwise in good shape and should be ok in a few days' time, I am really surprised he had such minor injuries; someone out there must have been watching over him?". As Declan turned to Jacqueline with a relieved look on his face, "Can we see our son now please". They bother entered Colm's room, he was making a lot of sense as he told his Mam that he had spoken to God, and he is ok for the Confirmation Day. Declan and Jacqueline looked at one another, a little confused themselves, Colm talking of God? Declan muttered to Jacqueline, "I think Colm probably still a bit delirious". Colm whispered to his dad, "No, I talked to God at the Buoy, and it worked out fine. I am good to go with a big smile on his face.

Declan and Jacqueline walked towards the Nurses' station to have a word with the Doctor to see if everything was ok with Colm's condition. Dr Richards informed them that Colm was doing great, he said, "he is a strong lad, with a strong character". Jacqueline smiled with a joyful look on her face, "yes, he is like his dad". Colm would be discharged in a couple of days, as Dr Richards did not envisage any problems. Declan and Jacqueline headed home to let the girls know the good news.

Hand in hand, Declan and Jacqueline walked towards the car park, as Delcan got into the car, he turned his head to Jacqueline, "Let's take the scenic route home and drive through Seaburn; the sun still has a glimmer of sunshine, how perfectly lovely, it's passed teatime? I have never known such a beautiful sky at this time of the day? and all is good with the world". Jacqueline replied, "You are right my love, the sky has never looked so beautiful … Seaburn and its white sandy beach and lovely Tea Rooms even in the winter months. Joggers out, dog walkers out, it's a vibrant coastline full of life. It's always a breath of fresh air to just step out and feel the sea air and salty aroma, heavenly bliss.

Home again, as the evening started to draw in Declan got changed and headed to the colliery, as he had unfinished work to attend to. Niamh and Emily skipped merrily upstairs to listen to the radio. Jacqueline didn't take her brown duffle coat off, she walked down to the Beach and sat in her favourite spot, a little alcove, her favourite rock at Trow Rocks to reflect and sometimes prayer. She could let her emotions out and even have a little cry for Jacqueline was emotional and sensitive at times, but always strong and focused when she had to me. The sun was shining it was a very cold breeze and the sky was blue, the seagulls were happy to sit around the rocks. As Jacqueline looked up at them, she said to herself, "what a beautiful sight; they are like sand dancers tipping and flapping about, that squawking song they love to sing". Jacqueline just sunk herself into the world of nature and its serene presence even though it was cold, but this doesn't get the chores done. Back up the hill, into the back gate, washing and ironing to be done.... Radio 4 on. listening to the play, "a picture of Autumn".

The week went by with little drama, it was Colm's homecoming, and his favourite tea was on the table for him, Fish, Chips, plenty of batter and mush peas. Colm was asking if he will be able attend the Cup Final on Saturday as United were playing. Declan had tickets well advance for them. He waited with bated breath until his dad came home to discuss it. The door opened… Colm was first to the door asking his dad, "we are going to the final dad?" Declan replied, "we are lad! we are!" Declan and Colm loved United, and nothing would deter them away from such a special day….

The day had come Colm was up early getting his black and white strip ready to wear, with his famous black and white wooden rattle. Declan wore his black and white shirt and cap. The pair of them were buzzing, Jacqueline and the girls were looking on with pride. They would take the ferry over to North Shields and catch a bus into town as Declan thought it would a disaster driving into town. The ferry only takes 7 mins across to North Shields and there are a few buses to choose from to get into town. Yes, he thought, that is a good plan. United won on aggregate 6:2 the whole town was illuminated with pride and joy as they took to the streets to see the players on the open top bus with the Cup. Thousands cheering on… what a day to remember…

Saturday night and Declan and Colm still dressed in their black and white shirts, and caps! "Caps off lads! At the table as Jacqueline gave them a scowling look as she had prepared homemade food; Quiche, corned beef pie, sausage rolls and roast beef and chicken sandwiches, and Declan's favourite bacon and egg pie. For dessert a homemade Trifle. Declan shouted out, it's time to put the radiogram! On! which LP's or singles to you want, requests now before I choose the lot. Niamh, I want the four Tops, 'I'll be there' and Diana Ross 'Stoned Love'. Emily spoke out and requested 'the Elgins, 'Heaven must have sent you'. The boys had their favourites, the Beatles, 'Hey Jude', Jacqueline was a big fan of soul music and loved the Beatles too, she was pleased with any of them. They all sang along danced away until 10.00pm. Declan went to the cabinet and brought out his special occasion Whiskey, he loved a wee dram on special occasions, and Jacqueline loved Ginger Wine. The girls and Colm had their favourite lemonade. Declan's brother Dylan arrived to join in and some of neighbours as it was a friendly neighbourhood, and everyone knew everyone.

Declan and Dylan sat in the kitchen catching up with the day's events and reminiscing about the goals scored. Dylan always got carried away with football, being the younger brother by 10 years, his voice had gone, as he had been cheering and shouting incessantly at the game. It was Delcan who always had to keep his brother in check, to make sure he didn't get too enthusiastic and get himself into trouble.

They were both brought up in Ireland and it was when they were in their teens when they moved to Tyneside as their father Alistair was a Shipwright and due to the lack of jobs, he found employment at the Dry docks. It was Alistair's cousin David who wrote to him and told him the work was good in Tyneside. Dylan followed in his father's footsteps as a Shipwright, studying to be an engineer Declan was the mathematician as he became a manager down the pits. He was very diligent and fought for the safety equipment and regulations to be upgraded at every turn. He was well liked at Dunston Colliery. Even though they chose different paths, they stayed connected to one another with

Football being the major player in their lives. Declan and Dylan had too much whiskey that night as they stayed up until the early hours.

It's going to a hell of hangover Jacqueline was saying to herself as she finally got to sleep.

Chapter 3

As the seasons started to change, it was getting more like spring every day. Jacqueline took a stroll down to the Beach before heading off to Mass. She left everyone in bed this fine Sunday morning, as she walked back to the cottage, she noticed the flowers were starting to bloom, yes, spring is nearly here. The sun was warmer than usual and glistened even more across the beach head. Spring she thought a time of hope and aspirations, she felt a poem coming on...

It's flow-like rustling, tightened stem...
The Rosebud quivers and lifts its arm, it moves with grace and blossoms like a sacred requiem...
for spring is an elevated sound, it lightens the soul... its pure essence smelt across the ground, for spring is the garden of dreams...it lingers and lingers; a substance that flickers all around that grassy beam that stood so close to the whimpering stream...

It was Jacqueline's favourite pastime, making up poems in an instance. She was almost late! for Mass! Just in time, phew.... Fr Donnelly gave a lovely sermon on Spring and changing of seasons, as Easter was around the corner and Confirmation time was due. He was looking forward to teatime at the Gibson's, as he loved Jacqueline's baking, his main reason for the trip to the Gibson's was to discuss Colm's Journey of Faith; that was not a priority in his mind as he finished Mass, but the rumblings in his tummy suggested that he was more than ready for the feast at the Gibson's, as Jacqueline was always over generous with the food, an attribute Fr Donnelly greatly appreciated.

Fr Donnelly was not your typical Irish priest he was in some ways unconventional as he didn't wear a Biretta Chasuble (the head piece) or the Cassock (the dress) he preferred his black suit and trilby. Everyone in South Shields liked him for that, he was a happy chappie always singing songs. His congregation was full

16

to the max at church, standing room only. Lots of people did stand and didn't mind.

Colm was all ready to face the music, Jacqueline and Declan were so impressed with Colm as he seemed to be taking his Confirmation so very well, he seems animated at times.... Fr Donnelly was happy to spell out the renewal of Faith to Colm, and as usual it is a lengthy process to go through the Journey of Faith. Everyone was taken back with Colm's enthusiasm to engage with the process. Fr Donnelly was enthused with the engagement, like he had never been before. It had turned out to be a grand day, with such lavish food, and an aminated audience, Fr Donnelly was inspired. Colm picked St Aiden as his Saint's name, as it was the catholic tradition to choose a Saint's name, a symbol of guidance and protection. Colm chose St Aiden an Irish Monk who founded a monastery on the Island of Lindisfarne, Holy Island. It seems Colm had done a bit of research into the Saints of Lindisfarne, as Colm loved Lindisfarne since a wee child, as the family used to go often, it has the most beautiful coastline, and a wonderful castle. A good walk-in sea at Holy Island was always a treat, shallow end of course. We all love to visit Lindisfarne.

Jacqueline and Aileen listened away at Father Donnelly's instructions, as they both turned to one another and smiled, "Fr Donnelly never altered in his speech or dedication to the forthcoming celebration of Confirmation. Aileen being the older sister and always happy to oblige Jacqueline with the kids, and she didn't have any children of her own, she wasn't inclined like most. She always said she was selfish and liked her independence. A career lady, who owned a Wool shop in the high street which kept her very busy, he was a very popular shop with lots of customers. Her husband Arthur was older than she and he was quite happy in the motor trade and was happy with their life together. They were always together when not working. and loved their house on the hill, it was their pride and joy, the dinner parties were a must for their clients and customers. An affluent couple who loved their holidays.

Tea was over, and the conversation turned to Emily who was looking to finishing school and joining her Aunt Aileen as a trainee in her Wool Shop. The excitement was showing in Emily's face as she loved making things, and the Wool Shop was not just a Wool Shop it covered other crafts such as tapestry and crochet. Emily was so very happy at the prospect of starting, a few weeks to go and she will be raring to go. Niamh was so happy for her. Emily is to receive £2 a week as a trainee and was adamant that she would pay her Mam and Dad £1 a week as she would now be a wage earner. Declan and Jacqueline were so proud of their Emily, but they wanted her to keep her money until the 6-month training was over. Emily was having none of it. Niamh was asking Emily if that meant to would get sixpence for sweets at the local shop. Colm said, "I probably get threepence because I am the youngest, the young bairn". Emily piped up, "you not having sweets, wait until you get a job". Colm winked at this sister, "I am winding you up Sis, I am waiting on a paper run from local newspaper, I am next in line, won't be long as he gave another wink back at this sister. Niamh was hard at it studying as she was coming up to 14 years old now and has set her sights on college, and hopefully a Saturday job in the local hairdressers to pay for some of the books. The Gibson children were all hard workers and not shy in getting on with it, they have taken a leaf out of their parent's book.

The conversation turned to Jacqueline who was explaining to Aileen about her new book club group she has started at the church social. Aileen said, "I knew you would do something like that – you and your books". Jacqueline was animated as there was so much interest and it was going so well too. The group would discuss a topic and pick a book out of the library annexed to the church social and they would all read and meet back in 2 weeks to discuss their thoughts and ideas. The first book was Rebecca by Daphne du Maurier.

Declan and Dylan went for their spritely walk along beach discussing life and all its demands, for all that they both loved their jobs and life as it was. Dylan was in between girlfriends and Declan was doing his best to get his brother settled down, but he was very reluctant, just hadn't met the right girl yet he said... Declan was advertising how great it was to be married and have children, Dylan was not opposed to marriage, but he wanted someone very special indeed, a perfectionist was Dylan... There were a few girls he introduced to the family, but Dylan didn't seem to be that enthusiastic after a few dates. Jacqueline thought Diane from the local Grocer's shop, a nice girl, she was the last one he brought around to see the family. Dylan thought she was a little bit boring, oh dear! as she would constantly talk about her life in the Grocers Shop. Dylan felt as if he knew everybody's business as Diane did tend to talk to all the customers. Jacqueline soon began to realise Dylan was quite right in his assumptions. Dylan is a tall brown hair man 6ft muscular and very sporty. He was looking for someone similar with a great sense of the outdoors and great personality, not to mention she must be extremely pretty, not too much to ask then.

The week went by so quickly, the mornings were brighter, and evenings were longer as spring was here and the air was light. Colm was fitted for his first suit of which he was not that keen at first, but started to feel quite at home with it, to Declan's surprise... Today was here Confirmation Day, and the Church was full to the prim, everyone turned out with their Sunday Best on. It was long service, but very moving. Bishop from Auckland attended the ceremony which was very Grand indeed. Everyone was in awe of the occasion.

There was a Marquee set out at the Beach for the afternoon festivities, music, dancing, and the local band turned out. It was a beautiful sunny day, and the sky was so blue. Aileen had organised the Marquee with a little help from her friends and the Church congregation chipped in too. It was organised so very well. Jacqueline and her friends, Lydia and Polly rallied round so everyone had a seat and everyone got a plate and a drink in their hand. There was always a little jealousy among some of the parishioners, but Jacqueline always did her best to include everyone, sometimes it was not always greatly appreciated, there was always trouble, namely, Gloria and Patricia who loved gossip, these pair could cause a riot in the nunnery! that's for

19

sure… Jacqueline was thick skinned and didn't let anything get her down in that way… Gloria had been spreading a rumour, that Jacqueline and Aileen had taken the table and chairs from the local furniture shop without permission for the day's events. In fact, Jack the owner of the furniture shop had donated the tables and chairs for the special occasion. Gloria was never taken seriously after that. It was always an upward battle at church as Gloria and Patricia had their own seat at church, as they would always say? and no one could sit in it, quite a few parishioners made the mistake of sitting in their seat … Fr Donnelly tried to be the peacemaker. but gave up.

Gloria and Patricia were not shy of grabbing the first opportunity to make their way to the food first, as Jacqueline glimpsed in their direction, "Oh, even the Marquee and the occasion hasn't stopped them from their usual habits on a Sunday, especially where the food is… Jacqueline winked across at Fr Donnelly and diverted his attention. He reciprocated with a roll of his left eyebrow; his expression was a picture.

Every Sunday when the congregation arrived, they all stayed clear of the third pew first two seats… with the exception when newcomers arrived. It was to be the highlight of some who didn't inform newcomers, they all loved the drama that is to follow… carrying on right through coffee morning. Quiet and peaceful at Church! not always the case at St Bernadette's in South Shields… Patricia and Gloria into battle every Sunday …. It's a drama in itself… everyone anticipating what will happen next… Fr Donnelly and his Irish humour always saves the day; he is ready for anything. He always makes the comment, "Patricia and Gloria are like a piece of art they draw their weapons with such pride".

The tables were set for coffee morning, let battle commence. Patricia heads to her table, Patricia designated the table to herself as it was the biggest and it had centre point for all the congregation to see first as they entered the hall. Patricia was off the mark once again to display her cakes and pastries. Gloria was fuming, but she wouldn't be defeated for she was hatching her own plan for further Sunday coffee mornings.

Fr Donnelly took his place in his usual chair way at the back, out of the way of any disputes, that was the way of Fr Donnelly, anything for peace and quiet while he ate the delicious pastries. He wasn't left alone for long though, as Fr Donnelly always found his exit as soon as he finished his pastries he would jump up and say his goodbyes very swiftly as he smirked through the door to his quarters. He gasped a sigh of relief when he shut his front door, he had Oscar his cocker spaniel eagerly awaiting his return as Oscar would leap upon him, "Time for your feed I think Oscar", as Fr whistled away into the kitchen.

Meanwhile in the hall Jacqueline simmered everyone down to announce the raffle prizes, as the raffle monies was going towards the church roof that needed some attendance. Gloria had won to her delight a box of chocolates; Patricia gave her usual look of not being very happy at all about that. "She always comes up smelling of roses that one".

Sunday mornings at Church always finished on a happy note, and Jacqueline was happy with the prospect of having raised £100 for the roof fund. Happy days, as she smiled to herself.

Chapter 4

After a lively weekend, the elevation of nature had come to embrace us as the beautiful flowers and trees had started to grow into their own. Jacqueline took to her patch of garden to tidy up the scrubs and admire the beautiful roses and daffodils blowing in the wind. The week passed by as the hours turned into days, without an incident.

Friday came around so quickly, and Dylan was ready for his 'boy's night out' as he made his way to the new Italian Bistro, he had no idea he was going to meet the love of his life, he dressed to impress, as it was a new establishment and it is bound to be upmarket, not his usual Friday night out with the lads. Dylan was intrigued and quite excited about going to a new venue. The night didn't disappoint, and Dylan had met Serena, and couldn't stop thinking about this girl or talking about her. He just couldn't wait to have that conversation with his is brother as he always valued his big brother's opinion on everything.

As Dylan arrived at Declan's Jacqueline opened the door and was surprised to see Dylan so late at night? "Is Declan up? I need to talk to him, something so amazing has happened". Jacqueline shouted Declan who was just about to go to bed, "where is the fire brother, what time do you call this then?" They all made their way to the living room and Jacqueline put a pot of coffee on for everyone.

Dylan began to explain he had just come from the Italian Bistro where he had met Serena the most amazing girl but was talking so quickly Jacqueline had to get him to slow down, he was that excited. Declan pointed out to Dylan that the new bistro was usually a place where the professionals hang-out, like bankers, lawyers. Dylan with a wry smile said, "yep, I know, I wouldn't have gone, but Harry, Dylan's mate, an engineer who worked alongside Dylan at the Shipyard was insistent as the new band was in town and they were playing at the new venture. It was the best night our Bro, really was. Dylan went onto to tell his story about how he met Serena, 'a happy accident'. He was turning to hand Harry his drink and bumped into Serena, accidentally spilling some of lager over her! Serena was not impressed, Dylan was so devastated, he offered to pay for the dry cleaning, to compensate Dylan bought some very expensive cocktails for Serena and her friends. Serena was impressed with Dylan's approach, so assertive, taking charge, of clumsy situation, not bad looking either with a smile on her face. Serena and her friends invited Dylan and Harry to their table, and it was a night to remember.

As they sat around the table, Serena's friends made themselves scarce as it was obvious Serena was taken with Dylan's presence. Serena and Dylan talked all night about their ambitions, their views on life and their favourite things to do. Serena was taking her exams to be a qualified Solicitor; she was 25 years old. Dylan was 29 years old. They both had a lot in common, as they both loved the Beach, and loved swimming, not to mention the love of horses, and their daily run every morning. Dylan loved horses, but never had the occasion to learn to ride, maybe he will one day? Serena also, liked to ride, she had her own horse, as her family were from the legal sector and owned a small spread in Alnwick with stables. Dylan escorted Serena to her Taxi, and they exchanged telephone numbers.

The sunset seemed so early this morning, Dylan couldn't sleep, his thoughts were full of Serena, he had arranged to meet her the following Friday, as he got out of bed, he decided to look up the local restaurants, after all it will be their first date, and he was bit nervous about getting this right. He scoured the local directory, his thoughts were all over the place, "No, let's go for a farmhouse, nope, the beach, yes, the beach, fish, we both love fish. Yes, that's it, the best Fish at the Beach is Collette's…...It overlooks the sea, that's rather romantic" ... He sighed, "yes… sorted". Dylan began to get sleepy and lay on bed and went into a deep sleep. He awoke at noon, and went for a run along the beach, and stopped off at Declan's for a glass a water.

Jacqueline was intrigued by Dylan's new girlfriend, "tell us more about Serena". "Well, Serena is going to be a qualified Solicitor in 3 months, and her family are middle classed who live in Alnwick". Declan was taken back by this certain information, as he felt Serena maybe out of his league, but Jacqueline didn't believe in class division, according to Jacqueline, everyone washes from the same basin.

Niamh entered the room, "what's that about class Mam? "Oh, nothing hinny, just saying everyone is in the same class when it comes to breeding, if you are brought up right and value your life and possessions and are kind and generous to others you are in the same class as those who are born into money. For money is a dispersible asset that sometimes clouds people's judgment. Niamh replied, "Mam you are always tell it how it is, so honest, love you for that". Declan gave Jacqueline a loving look, and said, "yes Niamh your Mam is the be all and end all". They sat down around the fire and Niamh explained that she had an exam in English the next day. She had done her homework on, "Jane Eyre – Charlotte Bronte author".

Niamh's teacher had specifically outlined the aspect of the rich and poor and the social conditioning affecting the storyline. Niamh who was to write her composition on what affect did it have on Jane Eyre's spirit when entering Thornfield Hall. Niamh was excited about her composition as she loved Charlotte Bronte and was hoping to get her CSE with A grade. Niamh was doing well at school, and Jacqueline was convinced that she would achieve her goals, as she was always supported and thrived on Niamh's education, in her view, it was most important for children to go on and live their dream, it was her last year at school as she was coming up to 15 and college was all organised, St Swithin's College. Jacqueline had discussed this with Declan and the possibility of Niamh going to university as she was such a study bug. They had set aside monies for that prospect.

Jacqueline was immersed in Jane Eyre with Niamh for a moment and suddenly remembered the Book Club on Thursday and would re-read, "Rebecca" as the group would be discussing this novel in detail, no doubt some will have more to say than others, as Jacqueline was aware of some who would go over their 15 minute synopsis, mentioning no names, but Patricia and Gloria, who storm the church on Sunday, and unfortunately, were first on the list for the book club.. Jacqueline had her work cut out on Thursday. Lydia and Polly will quieten them down a touch, an extra 15 minutes will be needed to restore order, Jacqueline smiled to herself; an eventful evening it will be....

Emily entered the room she was full of beans loving her first job at the wool shop. Aileen, Jacqueline's sister was happy that her Wool Shop was in good hands, she was pleased with the way Emily was handling the customers being so friendly and helpful and assisting them on how to choose the right wool for the right pattern. Some of stories Emily would come home and tell, it was like she knew everyone's personal life as they would divulge their day, for instance, Mrs Cragg a regular would come in and tell Emily about her life, her daughter Betsy who looks after her who is a national treasure. Emily was so attentive and very astute, as she would point out to Mrs Cragg at times, "oh Mrs Cragg the queue is getting a bit big, so I must attend to other customers". Emily always did it in style not to offend the customers, she certainly was a natural.

Colm came running in from the wet outside, he had been playing football. Declan told him upstairs get dried off son and made him a hot chocolate. Colm was getting into his stride with his paper round, he was enjoying that small bit on pocket money; a shilling a week to deliver the papers with assistance of course, it was a start, and he valued his shilling a week and saved it up. He now had £2 in his piggy bank. Declan and Jacqueline were proud of the way their children had become such carers of their possessions. He had set his sights on buying an Art and Craft Set, as Colm loves to draw the seagulls at the Beach. Declan was hoping that Colm may one day follow in his footsteps to become a trainee draughtsman. Colm was not that forthcoming as he was too busy with his mates, playing football, and looking out for more adventure.

Colm wasn't academically studious, but he was enthusiastic about drawings and how to work them out, as maths was his best subject at school, he hated reading, he found it very boring. He certainly didn't take after his mother and sister Niamh. Colm was his Father's Son in a lot of ways.

Thursday had arrived, Jacqueline was bracing herself for the Book Club get together. She sighed, if only we could have a night without Patricia and Gloria, how interesting it would be she thought. Aw well, let's get to the Church Centre, and set up. Everyone had arrived, in Patricia and Gloria. Jacqueline made it quite clear that everyone would have their chance to comment on the book for the month, "Rebecca". We will start from right to left, so Lydia, first, followed by Polly, Lucy, Christine, Patricia, and Gloria. Patricia and Gloria looked at one another and whispered, "that's not fair why are we last, Lydia ooh Teacher's pet!".

Lydia began with saying that she thought the book was about a young woman who is shy but becomes so impetuous and turns out to be the heroine who finds strength and courage to overcome her fears. She had plenty of fears especially with the housekeeper Mrs Danvers. It's a very gothic novel, dystopian in nature, given the effect that the first Mrs De Winter is haunting Manderley the home of the De Winters. I loved the flash backs from the past I think it gives out that haunting image right from the start; the reader gets hooked from page one. I loved it, especially the twist when Mr De Winter informs the second Mrs De Winter that he never loved Rebecca, he never had a moment of happiness with her, so dramatic... Jacqueline thanked Lydia, for her lovely observations, which everyone loved, except Patricia and Gloria, they never seem to appreciate other people's comments....

It was Polly's turn to outline her thoughts. Polly found Mr De Winter rather cold and calculating in the first instance. It's easy to see that the narrator, who becomes the second Mrs De Winter was imprisoned initially by her companion and then goes on to be captivated by Mr De Winter. The storyline is riveting Polly went onto to say as Mr De Winter tries to steer his dark haunting moods of the past from his memory, Rebecca seems to haunt him all the way through the novel. He goes on to pacify himself by connecting to the unnamed character in the novel (the second Mrs DeWinter) who he meets in the foyer of the Hotel where they are staying, who is a total contrast to Rebecca, she is plain, and very shy. It's great novel about love and hate and how they combine to bring about good prevails over evil in the end, "Thank you, Polly,", Jacqueline replied. Lovely observation.

Lucy and Christine were of the same view as Lydia and Polly and added that they loved the second Mrs DeWinter at the beginning of the Novel and the iconic headlines, "Last night I dreamt I went to Manderley again". They found it so interesting and the fact that the author wouldn't give the name of the Second Mrs De Winter, maybe because she was the worthy one of the De Winters? Patricia and Gloria's thoughts were that of Rebecca being a dark romantic tale, and they didn't really like the story line at all, they would prefer a more upbeat book with a lot of gossip and arguments in it.... It turned out they had not really read the book at all.... Jacqueline pointed out that the Book Club conditions were that you were to read the whole book, even if you found it not to your taste. Patricia and Gloria stood up, "Well! I think Gloria and I will leave it at that thank you! I don't think this is for us, hey! Gloria!". Gloria replied, come on Patricia, let's get down the pub, where we are welcome". They left... Jacqueline and the other members stood up and clapped and hugged each other. 'We have our book club back, yes! Jacqueline shouted!

Chapter 5

Dylan was fast approaching his big date night. Harry his best friend was rather dubious about it becoming a regular thing, as Harry had this feeling his best friend is about to get hurt for the first time in his life. He was secretly hoping that it turned out he was wrong, only time will tell he thought…. He hadn't seen his best friend so animated and alive. "Well, Dylan, you ready for your big night, enjoy bud". Dylan looked towards this best friend, "I am so looking forward to this night", as they stepped off the gang plank at the shipyard having just finished, they stint of erecting a new engine in a boat that sailed into dock from Auckland. They were pals from the first day they met on deck 5 years gone, when they are were selected to erect the piping below on a new ship that was being built, "the Oregon". Their first ever venture on a new ship, Dylan, and Harry inseparable after that.

As the conversation turned to Harry and his longtime girlfriend Isla, "you are all set up though, aren't you?" "It's about time I waited long enough, as Harry gave Dylan that cheeky smile; "strong words bud from a man who has been so casual with the girls", I will wait until you have had 5 dates, then I will make my mind up ha ha "…. Dylan laughed out loudly, "You will see I am right, I am always right", as they made their way to the cars. It was a half hour drive home for Dylan as he lived not far away from his brother Declan in a one-bedroom apartment overlooking the sea, their daily chats always involved the long walk along the beach, that sorted out anything that was troubling them….

Dylan was all set in his best polo shirt and brown slacks, very polished brown brogues. He shaved a bit too much and nicked his left jaw slightly, which annoyed him immensely … He had a 15-minute walk to the beach end where Collette's Fish restaurant was, it was a restaurant that had full glass images so that you can eat and take in the very special view of the silky sand and gushing waves, not to mention the lighthouse just a mile to the left. On the right you could see Trow Rocks at a distance. He was early, a half hour early, it was coming up to April and the nights were light, the sea was calm there were plenty of stars in the sky tonight. "Maybe I should wish on one", he thought… As he stared into the sea waves watching the Ferry go by with the local passengers aboard, he felt a tap on his back, it was Serena, she looked lovely in her blue top and navy slacks, and cream slip-ons. Serena had long brown hair, it was set up in a bun style with a cream scarf that was wrapped around above her fringe and tied at the back. She looked elegantly tall at 5ft 6 inches, with her slim build. Dylan just looked at her big brown eyes and thought, "how lucky am I?" …

They both entered the restaurant, he had booked a table just in case, he didn't want anything to go wrong. They were seated at the front, Serena, commented on the view and was so impressed. She said, "my goodness I have never been to a fish restaurant by the sea". Dylan replied, "it's the best place to be". Dylan ordered a lager for himself and a Manhattan cocktail, as he now knew it was Serena's favourite. The night had got off to a good start, as they tucked into their fish dish, Dylan had the big fish platter, and Serena had the traditional Fish with chips, she was blown away, "Wow! she said, this is amazing fish, I shall definitely be coming here again". Dylan loved her well-spoken manner and enthusiasm. They had covered everything from films, music, hobbies, and even they little idiosyncrasies… Serena went onto say how she is very neat and tidy and folds everything… Tidy mind, "clutter creates chaos ", she said… Dylan laughed, "Aw well lovely lady, I am reasonably tidy, I do have a habit of hiding things like under bed", as he cheekily grinned back at Serena.

They talked of the weekend and Dylan explained that it was Declan's 40th birthday on Sunday and there will be a party, a Marquee would be set up on the Beach for a family and friends gathering. I know this is probably a bit presumptuous of me as we haven't known each other for that long, but I feel like I already got to know you well already, would you like to come along? Serena happily smiled back at Dylan, "I would love to come", then that's settled. I will pick you up at 2pm on Sunday, Serena realised at that moment that Dylan was going to be at her home... and she quickly thought, I must do a quick introduction to Mum and Dad and then we can be off she thought, good thinking.... Dylan then realising that this would be the first time he would be going to Serena's ... They continued with the rest of the meal and ordered a lovely dessert, Chocolate Tarte with Ice Cream.

It was lovely night and stars were out, they both looked down at the beach and waves through the glass window, the night was still, like a romantic setting in a film Serena thought... Dylan remarked on how the sea was so calm and would Serena like to stroll along the beach. Serena replied, "I was thinking the same thing" ... They strolled down the pathway, took off their shoes, and Dylan grabbed Serena's hand they walked along the long stretch of beach. They noticed the lifeboats far out on their usual patrols. "This beach is like a beautiful haven", Serena said. Dylan remarked, "Yes, it has its moments, but come the summer season when all the donkey rides are in force and all the beach huts are in business, it's a buzzing atmosphere", nights like tonight are when you can see the absolute beauty of the sea and rocks and the silky sand. Serena looked surprised! "Dylan, how poetic of you, I didn't know you were into poetry?". I think I am picking up some tips from the sister-in-law Jacqueline she is so poetic and quite good at poetry. I do like a good read and admire writings of beauty and landscape. I believe that is why I wanted to work on ships, the beauty of the craftmanship and how it looks so prominent on the sea once a ship finished. Serena was liking Dylan even more as they held hands and walked along the sandy beach.

The wind was started to pick up fast, Dylan put his jacket around Serena's shoulders, they looked like two silhouettes from a distance. Dylan wished he hadn't had a drink now as he could have taken Serena home. On second thoughts, I will escort her in the taxi, forget the cost, it's well worth it. As they continued their stroll towards the lighthouse, Dylan turned to Serena and became locked in each other arms for what seemed an age, Serena wanted to come up for air! They arrived at the lighthouse; a picturesque frame of pure art; a pillar of the sea, as it stood up a like a gleaming protector. They sat and admired its' image. It was getting late, and they headed back. "I will see you all the way home lovely lady ". Serena was shocked, "You are forgetting for a minute I live in Alnwick! it will cost you a fortune there and back", I am paying half". Dylan was not having that, a woman paying half, not on my watch ever!

They got into the taxi huddled in each other arms. The journey seems so short they both thought as they didn't want it to end. The taxi pulled outside Serena's home a 4 bedroomed Cottage style house, beautiful landscape garden. Dylan got out of the taxi to wish Serena good night, they lovingly kissed, and Dylan raced into the cab before Serena could reach her bag, he shouted "See you Sunday beautiful at 2pm and blew a kiss". Serena was so impressed with his manly ways and smiled and waved and went into the house.

Saturday arrived, Jacqueline was feeling very curious about Serena, "Don't forget to get all the info on Serena", Jacqueline prompted Dylan. Declan reminded Jacqueline that Colm was coming along too. "Ooh Declan why should that matter?", Jacqueline said. Dylan pointed out to Jacqueline, "It does, can I just say, the reason being that it's grown-up talk, and Colm has just had his 11th birthday, and we will be concentrating on the match". Take Dylan to the pub when you drop off Colm, why don't you? Jacqueline replied. "Well if You put it like that pet, then, yes, that is a great idea, that is the first time you have forced me into the pub", Declan laughed loudly. "I know, may God forgive for that". Jacqueline smiled, and grabbed her crucifix around her neck and gently swung side to side on her neck, she often did that when she felt she needed that assurance it wasn't such a bad thing, was it?

Dylan had arrived and Jacqueline swiftly moved towards Dylan, "Did you have good night last night Dylan" she asked. "It was grand thanks for asking" Dylan replied. That was all Jacqueline was going to get out of Dylan as Declan moved in quickly and got Dylan out the door and into the car. Jacqueline was very disappointed she didn't get the chance to ask Dylan more….

Colm was excited about the match and the game was as good as it could get a 5-nil victory for the Toon. They were in great spirits coming home. Colm ran into the house shouting, "Mam we won 5 nil Mam! It was so electric Mam you should have heard all the fans with their football rattles in the air Mam, it was like a massive Brass Band coming together!". "I bet it was! More like everyone screeching I would think, Jacqueline smirked, so glad you had a good time Son". Colm was starving, he had his favourite fish and chips for tea. Declan and Dylan went off the pub, Jacqueline winked at Declan, and he winked back.

Declan ad Dylan arrived at the Seashell pub, "A pie and pint I think is in order ", was Declan's response to a great day of football. "Oh yeah, bro, chips too", Dylan replied. They sat in their usual booth which has a view through the window of the crag end of which slopes into a beach cove.

Dylan began the conversation by explaining to Declan that he will be meeting Serena at his 40th Birthday bash. Declan was really shocked and surprised, "Wow young bro, you are certainly hooked!". "Hooked line and sinker bro", Dylan replied. "Jacqueline will be pleased", Declan smirked at Dylan. "Aww right, yes, I thought she was anchoring for a big conversation before you dragged me out the door, ha ha ". "I reckon you will be a wee bit nervous bro", Declan cheekily smiled at the corner of his mouth. "I am more nervous about picking Serena up tomorrow and meeting her folks to be honest". "Mmm, I bet, be yourself bro, you will be fine", Declan replied.

Chapter 6

Sunday morning arrived, Jacqueline was up at the crack of dawn, organising everything for Declan's big birthday. Unfortunately for Jacqueline she had forgotten she was to do the first reading at church this week. Jacqueline gave out a big sigh! As she knew Patricia and Gloria would not be amused as they usually do the readings. "I must have a word with Father before Mass today, and exclude myself", Jacqueline muttered to herself. The conversation with Father Donnelly went well, Jacqueline was relieved, as was Fr Donnelly if the truth be known...

It was a glorious springtime day. The children were looking forward to their dad's big birthday, Colm got him a black and white cap. Niamh and Emily bought him a watch together. Jacqueline subsidised them all for this auspicious occasion. Jacqueline bought her Declan his favourite Fred Perry shirt, with a dressy shirt and tie for the special day, his favourite blue herringbone classic shirt with matching tie.

Dylan was all set for his journey to Serena's, "I hope I look presentable enough", he whispered to himself... Dylan was wearing a shirt and tie, he wasn't a shirt and tie man like his brother Declan, but always wore them on special occasions, as his brother always pointed out to him, "If you want to look dapper bro, wear a shirt and tie", Declan's motto... Dylan looked dapper in his Navy suit and white shirt, he had borrowed Declan's blue Tie, "Now there is a first", as smirked at himself in the mirror. He had polished his black brogues that much he could see his reflection through them...

Serena was pacing up and down in her room looking out of the windows every second as walked past the window. Serena's Mam came into the room, "You will wear the carpet out girl, pacing like that, don't worry about your father, I will sort him out". Serena was dressed in her new polka dot dress, and classic boots, and wearing her hair down for a change she thought, with

33

an accessory, matching polka dot scarf which swooped her hair off her face. Serena's Mum (Charlotte) looked at her beautiful daughter and said, "You look amazing love". "I must take after you then Mum", Serena replied. They were very much like in looks and mannerism. Serena's Dad (Jonathan Inskip) was a very pompous man, a Commercial Lawyer. For Serena was his pride and joy and was very protective of her, which will be a big challenge for Dylan, as he is about to find out.

Dylan pulled up in is very shiny Austin Morris motor car, he had been cleaning it all morning... He rang the doorbell. It was Mr Inksip that answered the door, Dylan put his hand out to Mr Inskip thinking it was the right thing to do, but Mr Inskip turned and said, "Come in Mr Gibson I take it". Dylan looked a bit nervous and said, "Please call me Dylan", Mr Inskip stepped back and walked towards the staircase and raised his voice slightly as he called out to Serena, "Serena, Mr Gibson is here". Serena's father was not happy to associate himself with a Shipyard Engineer. Serena's Mum was very happy to shake Dylan's hand and escort him into the drawing room. "We are not stopping Mum", Serena replied, as we must get to the party and time is getting on". Charlotte, sighed, oh, I see, ok, then you are welcome to come to dinner next Saturday Dylan". A gasp and a pause from Dylan, "I would be delighted to Mrs Inskip". "Please call me Charlotte". "Thank you, Charlotte, Dylan replied". At that moment Mr Inskip arrived in the room with no idea of what had just transpired. A short silence as everyone looked at one another, Serena was the first to speak, "We need to be heading off now". Dylan smiled and shook Mrs Inskip's hand and said, "It was lovely to meet you". Mrs Inskip replied, "It's been a pleasure to have met you too Dylan". Mr Inskip moved forward and reluctantly shook Dylan's hand... Dylan turned to Serena, and they were out of the door, as he walked to the car, he gave out a big sigh and said, "That was tough, your father is not a fan of mine, not yet anyways". Serena looked a little subdued and replied, "He was rude, and I am not happy about that, and I will be telling him so later". Dylan was not having that as she turned to Serena and said "No! don't I rather you didn't, I would much rather win him over in my own time. They left it at that and drove to the Beach, and the car radio was playing a Matt Monro song, 'Portrait of my love". Dylan looked at Serena and knew at that moment that no matter what happens between them; they will eventually end up with each other, that was his plan, and he was sticking to it.

They finally arrived at the Beach, the Marquee looked fabulous, the family had already arrived. It was a beautiful day, breezy, but not a cold wind. The Marquee was situated not too far on the sand, it was near the cove, as Jaqueline was concerned some would prefer to leave their shoes, or sandals on... Jacqueline had organised for sand liners to be placed in the Marquee. Declan's best friend Tom and his family had arrived. Declan had invited Harry, Dylan's best friend and his partner Isla. There were lots of cousins and distant cousins and their friends. Declan hadn't got a clue who half of them were.

Dylan took off his shoes and Serena was more than happy to take off her boots, they both liked the feel of the sand on their feet. Jacqueline approached Dylan and introductions were made, as Jacqueline shook hands with Serena, she couldn't help but notice how well-spoken Serena was, it put her out of step for a moment. Declan arrived to say hello, he too was taken back a little too, "A woman of class".

Niamh and Emily were next up and went to hug their uncle Dylan and said a shy hello to Serena. Niamh couldn't help herself, "I love your polka dot dress", it's fab. "I got this from town, I bet they have your size in it too", Niamh turned to Serena with a look of awe on her face, "It looks far too classy for me I think", "Oh, don't be silly, if you want to go shopping anytime, just let me know". Niamh shoulders went back with astonishment, as she felt a little overcome by the comment and simply nodded back with a faint smile.

Emily was not that into fashion or hair, she was happy with her wool patterns and crochet, not realising that it was fashionable to create garments out of wool. Emily was in world of her own. Colm came over to say hello to his favourite Uncle

Dylan and said a quick hello to Serena as he ventured over to his dad, "I have never seen Uncle Dylan with a girl before dad?". "Yes, it's a first Colm, Declan replied. "He must like her a lot then dad". "I would imagine so son", Declan smirked as he walked towards Jacqueline, they both sat down and started to talk about Serena. Jacqueline looked at Declan and said, "Serena is well bred, I am dying to know how Dylan went on at Serena's house?". Declan responded, "We will know soon enough pet, let's enjoy the party first".

The food was all laid out with plenty to drink for everyone. Serena went over to Jacqueline and asked who had done all this lovely food. Jacqueline stood back with amazement and said, "it was mostly myself and my sister Aileen with a few from church who pitched in. "Well, I think your roast beef sandwiches are amazing" as Serena tucked in. Jacqueline pointed out "they are made from roast beef joints slowly cooked in the oven; Aileen loves to bake cakes so help yourself Serena". Jacqueline was warming to Serena even with her well-spoken manner.

The presents were opened, and Declan made a short speech to everyone, given the coercion from everyone chanting his name, "Speech! Speech", it was now time for some live music. Tom Declan's dear friend had his guitar he was an ardent player in his spare time. Cousin Jack had his saxophone and Arthur, Aileen's husband on the harmonica. The music was very blues and soul which Declan loved so much. The day was turning out to be a great 40th, Declan thought to himself.

Serena and Dylan were huddled together near the cove and Serena pointed out that Dylan had a lovely warm family, and she hadn't enjoyed a day at the beach so much as she had today. Dylan was surprised at Serena, as he listened away to Serena, he had imagined Serena having fabulous days out in very upmarket surroundings. She was not a person who took wealth and status as a commodity that needs to be upheld, she was more of a person who does like nice things, but she would never call herself a snob. She was a down to earth rich girl. They both turned to one another, and Serena noticed that Dylan was not drinking any alcohol, Dylan pointed out that he would be driving her home, and she would not be getting a taxi. Jacqueline suggested that Serena stay at their beach house along the coast it's 5 minutes away, that would make more sense. Dylan turned to Serena and said, "What about your parents Serena?". "Can I telephone them from your cottage Jacqueline?". "of course, you can", Jacqueline replied. It was settled then they can now all relax and enjoy the evening.

Serena called, her father answered, he was furious, and demanded she get a taxi home. "I will most certainly not father, I am 25 years old, I am not a child!" Serena slammed the telephone down. Serena's mother was furious with her husband, "Will you stop! Meddling in Serena's personal life! she is a young lady who knows are to act in a proper manner, you should trust her!".

Back at the beach, Dylan was getting a little concerned that Serena was taking a long time to return; she suddenly appeared looking rather flustered, Dylan grabbed her hand and said, "Are you ok? it's your father, isn't it?". "Yes, he will soon realise I am now grown up, as its going to happen more often", Serena replied. Dylan was very happy with that remark. They all settled down to more rhythm and blues and Dylan relaxed with his glass of whiskey.

As the night ended Dylan escorted Serena to the beach house. They both embraced and passionately and kissed each other for some time. Dylan was aware they were alone in the beach house, and he was not going to be staying the night, oh no he thought, that comes later, as much as I want to I will not he whispered to himself. Serena was a bit nervous being on her own, but she wasn't showing it. She was very impressed with Dylan's manner, as much as she wanted him to stay, she too was thinking it's too soon, later when the time is right. They were both on the same wavelength when it came to acting in a proper manner. In that instance, they were both brought up as equal …

Dylan went up to the cottage to Jacqueline and Dylan and he told them all about the day at Serena's and the telephone conversation with her father. Declan pointed out that he will have his work cut out with Mr Inskip and Jacqueline pointed out that Serena is a woman with her own mind. Jacqueline told Dylan that he has a gem on his hands with Serena and they look great together. The conversation flowed for a few more hours and Dylan decided to stay on the sofa for the night, he was all done in and very happy with the day's events, he was up very early 6am, as it was a Monday morning, he had to get Serena back before 9 as it was a workday and he was on shift at 9am. Serena hadn't slept that great and was not looking forward to a day at the office, but she would never shy away from work. Serena's father came out to greet her when she arrived, and she just walked straight passed him. Dylan waved and drove off to get himself changed for work. Serena got her suit out of the wardrobe and was dressed and out of the house by 8.30am, she was not in the mood for any confrontations this morning, she would deal with her father tonight. Serena's, mum hugged her and waved, "See you later love, have a good day".

It was hard day at the office for Serena, and she was not particularly looking forward to seeing her father on returning home. "Let's get on with this once in for all", she said to herself as she drove into the drive. Serena was not going to let her father get a word in. They both raised their voices, and it was concluded with a compromise as Serena's mum interceded. They were not a family that usually rowed a lot, so it was a very emotional time for all of them. Serena's father realised that the lad from South Shields was not going to go away, and he would try and live with this reluctant as he may be... Serena was relieved in a way as she was emotionally drained at this point.

The day ended with Serena talking to Dylan on the telephone, discussing her father's bad manners, and how they eventually came to a truce. Dylan wasn't convinced but was happy to receive such information.

An evening at the Inskip's had arrived, it turned out to be a revelation for Dylan. "I better wear a suit I think for this special occasion", he checked himself over in the mirror, one last look, right he said "table manners work from the outside with the cutlery, let's get that right at least" …

Dylan had arrived promptly, he was greeted by Serena, who looked beautiful in her blue dress with a peter pan collar so elegant he thought. Mr Inskip was cool with Dylan, but not too frosty, he quizzed Dylan thoroughly about his position as a Ship Engineer. Mr Inskip was very surprised that being an engineer was very technical and not for the fate hearted, he found Dylan to be very intelligent, of which was a big shock to him, as he always thought ship engineers were rather common. The night was not at all bad and Serena and Dylan were left in the garden after dinner. They strolled around the lovely grounds and their relationship seemed to go to a higher level, as they both looked so much in love.

Chapter 7

Dylan called his brother Declan to give him an update on his blossoming romance, as he knew Jacqueline would be hankering for some news… Declan interrupted Dylan, "I will have to sign off bro as I am up at the crack of dawn tomorrow, as I have lots of inspections to take care of before the lads come down in the cages". It was busy day for Declan and his team at the colliery. The booster fans seem to be working for the ventilation. The safety lamps were looking good. The belt conveyor was in place and working. Declan checked his demographics, and the coal seams were imminent, and the lads could start to eject the coal from the seams. The lads would dig out the coal from shafts 2 to 5, that would take the day and night shift to clear those shafts. They were a good crew, hard workers; a team who just got on with the task in hand. Tom, Declan's right-hand man, his best friend was keeping an eye of the coal seams, Declan was checking the electrics.

The face was a dark and dismal place underground, but the lads were always singing and having a good banter to keep them at it. Everyone knew their jobs and didn't hesitate to help one other if they were any temporary landslides, which occur sometimes when a seam has a bit of friction and falls, they knew the suspected dust barriers, and always seem to be able to rectify it before the friction was too much. All the cutting was completing as planned.

Declan went over to shaft 3 and noticed some roof dirt coming through far too much as he went to investigate, the seam caved in! and caused an explosion! Declan and four of his men were pushed back on to a girder where it collapsed and it landed on John (Patricia's husband), it hit Declan on the head, and they were both out of it. The alarm was raised! The other men were badly bruised, but not seriously injured. The onset of the explosion affected the adjacent seam, and a further explosion was happening, it was chaos! All the men were fighting for their lives, and at the same time, trying to help their mates out…

The Dunston Colliery had the Siren blowing it sounded like a big ship hooting from sea, but the village knew what it was, and you could see everyone running along the beach towards the colliery. Jacqueline telephoned the Coal Office, but it was constantly engaged, she fled to the colliery, and on her way, she could see Father Donnelly who was trying to calm everyone. Jacqueline had tunnel vision her only mission was to get to the pit head and find out what is happening as she got there, she could see ambulances, fireman and police. At this point Father Donnelly opened the Community Centre in readiness for all the families to come together. A tragedy had happened, and no one was thinking straight except Father Donnelly.

The Superintendent of the colliery was active and giving his knowledge of the pit to the fireman, and the Emergency Services had arrived on stand-by, there were also volunteers from the lifeboat rescue team who were eager to help too. It was waiting game and will be for some hours at least everyone was told. Flasks of tea and coffee were all organised and sleeping bags and blankets, there were tents erected as no one was going to go home tonight. Jacqueline had previously left a message at the school for her children to meet her at the colliery. They had arrived an hour later and brought blankets with them as they were aware of the tragedy.

Father Donnelly took care of the older congregation and set up temporary beds in the community centre. It was a team effort from everyone as this tragedy was not going to end well for some. Jacqueline kept on swinging her catholic cross from side to side on the neck and prayed like she had never prayed before. A small group of the ladies wanted to come together to all pray. Patricia was among them, she at this time was unaware that her husband John was one of them who could be seriously injured. She wasn't her bossy self as she usually is, but she looked timid and lost. Jacqueline sat with her alongside all the other ladies who had their husbands working that day, they all got out their rosary beads and prayed to Our Lady for strength.

It was getting dark, and the flood lights were brought in, it seems an age before the superintendent of the colliery came across to the chief fireman to get an update on the situation. The gangway to the front of the pit was slowly becoming unblocked. The manpower tripled as everyone wanted to help get the trapped men out. No one knew exactly how many men were trapped, but Jacqueline knew in her heart that Declan would be in the thick of it. It was a trying time for all concerned.

Father Donnelly was urging everyone to get some rest, "You won't be fit to receive your loved ones if you don't", he shouted out. Jacqueline was trying to get Patricia to take a nap. Gloria and the others from church were getting the sleeping bags ready to get everyone settled. It was the longest night in their entire lives. As the sun rose at 5am, Jacqueline felt a tap on her shoulder it was Dylan he was looking after Colm, Niamh, and Emily. Suddenly they could hear loud voices, as the fireman were urging people to stand back, "coming through!" they shouted! As Jacqueline looked up, some casualties were being brought out on a stretcher. The first one to come out was Tom, Declan's Foreman, he was badly hurt, Jacqueline went over to whisper to him, "Where is Declan?". Tom was not conscious, so she had no idea if Declan was ok or not. The next one was John! his face was covered with the blanket, the sign that he was dead! The fireman came over to Patricia and said, "I am so sorry for your loss! Patricia collapsed in a heap and Jacqueline urged Father Donnelly to come over. Father Donnelly read John the deceased his last rites and moved quickly to Patricia. There was no consoling, Patricia… There were four more men brought out, they were identified as they were the young lads who operated the conveyor belts, they were badly bruised, but looked like they would survive ok.

More hours passed, before there was any more movement at all…. It was midday before some more men were carried out on the stretchers… Then came Declan! He was unconscious and was taken to the hospital quickly! he sustained a bad injury to the head… Jacqueline went in the ambulance with him, and Dylan followed in his own car with the children...

Declan was taken to intensive care, where he underwent x rays. Unfortunately, Declan slipped into a coma and the Consultant was to wait the outcome before addressing the issue on whether to operate or not? It was the worst time for the Gibson Family. Jacqueline sat and held Declan's hand and would not let go. She talked and talked to him and sang to him. Jacqueline was willing him to open his eyes. "Open your eyes, Declan! talk to me why don't you!", she kept saying it repeatedly, well alright then if you want to have a small sleep then that's ok, I forgive you for that, but I won't forgive you if you don't wake up and talk to me and that is a promise Declan Gibson!". Dylan urged Jacqueline to take a break! "No! don't be ridiculous Dylan! He will want me here if he wakes up! She said in an abrupt manner. Dylan sighed and gave her a look and said, "You are being ridiculous, you won't be in a fit state to talk to him if you keep going on like this, you have been sitting here for 12 hours without a break, see sense for goodness' sake!". Jacqueline muttered "5 minutes to wash up and have a cup and tea and that's my offer Dylan". "Yes, boss, at least that's a break hinny, they both gave a quivering smile to one and another.

Dylan sat with Declan who was not breathing on his own but through the ventilator supplied. Declan started to talk about their nights out. "Hey Declan remember that night when we came out of the Fish bar near the beach, and you had a bit too much to drink and you decided you wanted to swim naked in the sea! And you did, we never told anyone, and I always remind you of that when I want to persuade you to do something you don't want to. Well Declan, I want you to get a wiggle on bro and come back to us asap do you hear me bro?" Dylan sighed, and prayed to God, which doesn't happen often with Dylan…

Jacqueline arrived back at the hospital to find Father Donnelly at Declan's bedside, he had come to offer his support and to say a few prayers. He sat and looked at Jacqueline, "You look so tired my dear, you need to get your head down for a few hours". "I can get my head down in the chair thank you Father and have forty winks here, I am not leaving my husband! I am not! Ok

43

Jacqueline, I know that tone, so I will leave you to it for now, I will pop back later tonight to see how you are getting on. Father Donnelly gave her a pat on the back when leaving.

It was long night, and no change the next day. Mr Charleston the Surgeon popped him to see how Declan was doing. He told Jacqueline that once the swelling on the brain came down, and regained consciousness he would be able to operate. Declan would need an operation as the x ray showed a mass on there and the centimetres that were recorded suggested that this mass needed to be removed, it was a delicate operation, but the surgeon was confident that Declan would benefit immensely from it. Jacqueline was in a trance and didn't really comprehend anything the surgeon was saying, all that was on Jacqueline's mind was the joy she would feel when Declan wakes up.

Dylan arrived early the next day to see how things were going, he was being the rock of the family, taking over from Declan, as he took the children to school and took time off work that week so he could be there for everyone. Jacqueline was so grateful to him. "Have you been in touch with Serena Dylan", Jacqueline asked. "No, I haven't had time to be honest, I am sure she has heard about the mine collapsing and will understand", Declan sighed. Jacqueline urged him to call her, but he was for some reason reluctant, it was like he had second thoughts, his feelings were so disrupted with the Declan being in a coma. Dylan just kept thinking in his mind about the difference in class between himself and Serena's family, especially Serena's Father, who would be delighted if he changed his mind… Dylan was at this moment confused it was as if he had been in the mining accident himself? He couldn't understand why he felt that way. He was very close to his brother and subconsciously he may be suffering from the thought of losing his brother? he was going through so many mixed emotions in his head right now. He would not be persuaded and was adamant about the situation.

"Declan's hand moved! Jacqueline shrieked, go get the Nurse Dylan". Dylan ran down the corridor shouting, "Nurse! Nurse! Come quickly! As the nurse entered the room, she swiftly called on the Doctor on call at that time and he was there within minutes. There was movement from Declan, and the Doctor explained that he would get Mr Charleston to come once he was out of theatre which would be within the hour. Jacqueline sat impatiently holding Declan's hand, his eyes weren't fully opened at this time but there was movement.

Mr Charleston arrived, and explained to Jacqueline and Dylan that he would take Declan down for another x ray and see where they were at; a few more tests he said and then we will have more to go on. Mr Charleston suggested they both go and stretch their legs and grab a bite to eat as it will be a couple of hours. "I will come find you in the restaurant ok".

Jacqueline had a walk around the grounds for half an hour and they made their way to the restaurant. He will be fine you know Jacqueline, as Declan put his hand around her shoulder, our rock as he called Declan is going be back with us before we know it. Jacqueline took great comfort from Dylan's words.

Eventually Mr Charleston arrived, he was very pleased to announce that Declan had recovered consciousness, and it was decided that the operation would take place tomorrow. You can see him now. Jacqueline was euphoric! to say the least! Declan nodded and gave out a faint smile. They sat with Declan he smiled, Jacqueline gave him a warm kiss and said Welcome back my love! Well dear reader, I wonder how this is going to turn out for them all…

Chapter 8

Serena was getting quite frantic, no message or call from Declan. Her Father wouldn't let up," I told you so, these people have no manners or etiquette", these were his words of wisdom to Serena. Charlotte was furious with her husband, "Will you stop being such an awful snob it's so unattractive". Jonathan was shocked at his wife's outburst. Serena ran out of the house in tears, "Why is this happening to me!", as she got into her car. She drove to Dylan's but there was no sign of him. Serena decided to make her way to Jacqueline's and again no answer. As she left the cottage a neighbour shouted, "They are all at the hospital". Of course, Serena said to herself why didn't I think of that, especially as she knew about the accident it was all over the radio and papers.

She went to reception to try and locate Dylan, but they were not giving out any information as she was not a relative, she was distraught and as she sat in the grounds. An hour went by, and she spotted Dylan's car, he was just about to leave, as Serena shouted, "Dylan". He turned around with a look of dread on his face. "Hi, what are you doing here?". "What am I doing here! you haven't been in touch for days, why didn't you call me? "I am sorry, it's been an awful time as you should know?" "Oh, I see I don't matter then!". I am not saying that but have a bit of compassion why don't you" Oh so you are saying I am selfish then, well I don't think a phone call is much to ask for, maybe my father is right about you. "Oh yeah!! I can imagine what he has been saying about me, you don't have to repeat it, I get it! Without further ado, Dylan sped off in anger and frustration, "How dare she be so arrogant and selfish, how dare she! that's that then! I am done with her! Serena stood in shock, "What did I just say! Why did I say that! why!" As she got into her car, she reflected on her outburst and sighed, "He could have called me though", I would have been there for him. As tears came down her face, that's that then.

Serena parked her car at home and her mother came out and saw Serena had been crying. They made their way into the garden and Serena explained all to her mother.! "Don't worry sweetheart, you know what they say, true love never runs smoothly". "Really Mother, well this true love has just crashed and burned I think". "Don't say that sweetheart, it's your first row, there will be more, so brace yourself, we all have bumpy rides and making up is the best of all. "I don't think it will be that easy Mother, as I told Dylan that my father maybe right about him". "You didn't! ooh sweetheart that was uncalled for. "I know". As Charlotte put her arm around her daughter she said, "Leave it for now let the dust settle for a while".

Back at the hospital, Declan was getting prepped for his operation and Mr Charleston was very confident that this would be a complete success. Jacqueline was trying to feed off his confidence but would be so happy when it's all over. Dylan had arrived he looked awful as he hadn't slept a wink after the row with Serena. He just didn't have the heart to mention it to Jacqueline, he was determined to shut Serena out of his life, but he was doing a good job of it.

Declan came out of surgery and Mr Charleston explained that it was not as bad as anticipated as the mass had shrunk miraculously, he couldn't put his finger on it, but he thought that divine intervention may have stepped in, and Declan would have a full recovery. Declan would be out of action for at least a couple of months to recuperate. TLC then Jacqueline thought, I can do that as she beamed with joy. "When can my husband come home?", Jacqueline asks the Consultant. He replied with a hesitant look, "It will not be for at least 2 weeks, he has just come out of surgery, so we do need to keep a close eye on him for the time being". "I thought you said he would make a full recovery?", as Jacqueline answered the Consultant with a pensive look. "I am not saying he will not make a full recovery, what I am saying is the operation went well, and there were no malignancies, and I am confident he will make a full recovery, but recovery takes time as it was a delicate operation, I hope that makes more sense to you Mrs Gibson".

"Of course,", Jacqueline replied with a big smile on her face, "It does now, thank you so much". "I apologise for not being more open with you", Mr Charleston looked rather embarrassed as he said it, it was not like him to not clarify the matter fully. He seemed to be distracted by Jacqueline's beauty. Jacqueline had dark eyes and her flawless skin seem to captivate the Surgeon's attention, he was not being himself. Jacqueline hadn't noticed a thing as she was so delighted that Declan was to recover and she didn't mind about Declan being in hospital, for what is two weeks, when we have a lifetime to get through as she smiled lovingly at Declan. Mr Charleston then left the room feeling too embarrassed to stay. As he walked down the corridor, he was furious with himself, "What the hell is wrong with me ", he asked himself. I will never be so distracted again as he went back on his ward round smirking, really! a married woman distracts you, nope, I don't do that…

Dylan and the children arrived; they were so relieved about the good news. Declan needed a good rest, but he was reluctant to shut his eyes, as he wanted to see his children so much, he struggled to keep his eyes open, and eventually he went back to sleep, as they all sat around Declan's bedside and cuddled each other, watching their dad sleep.

Jacqueline took Dylan aside to have a talk with him; he looked so drawn in the face, as she tried to probe Dylan about Serena, he was reluctant to talk about it, but Jacqueline could tell by the fraught look on his face that all was not well with him. Jacqueline respected his wishes and changed the subject back to Declan and the awful events that took place at the mine. They sat together for some time and Dylan began to speak a little more freely about Serena. Jacqueline listened with concern, and her response to Dylan was that of, "Don't do anything hasty yet, just let things settled down a bit". Dylan was regretting his outburst, but he knew Jacqueline was making sense as he couldn't deal with any more emotional disturbances; Declan's recovery was far more important than anything else. He couldn't wait to get back to work to keep his mind occupied.

They all arrived home, and Dylan returned to work. The aftermath hit Jacqueline and it was announced that there were 14 dead from the explosion and there would be a vigil at the beach that night. It was an awful time for all concerned. There were to be 14 paper lanterns gliding out to sea to pay tribute to those who lost their lives. Jacqueline telephoned Father Donnelly to see if she could help at the Community Centre. As Jacqueline ventured to the Community Centre she bumped into Gloria and Lydia who explained Patricia was so very distraught, and they were keeping an eye on her even though they were not close. The disaster had certainly brought them closer together, and Jacqueline was relieved to see that they were all getting along together.

It was 7pm and they all made their way to the beach, it was a cool night just before Easter and the breeze was not too bad; There were fourteen paper lanterns glided over the sea to commiserate the lost souls, it was if they are dancing on air, it was a moving sight. Father Donnelly started the liturgy and Jacqueline had written a small poem to commemorate those lost souls:

The trickling echoes of our loved ones are real..
They seep into our hearts like a captivated seal..
For the echoes will go on and on …..
         and we will remember them with a happy song…

Father Donnelly picked out a fitting hymn for the heroes who had lost their lives. 'Love Divine, All Loves Excelling". It epitomises the joy of life and strengthens those who are suffering. It did help those in that moment. It was going to be a long journey of grieving for those who have lost a dear one. The togetherness was apparent, and everyone was supporting one and another, except one of the parishioners, Patricia who came over to Jacqueline and said, "I see your husband is alive!", how could that happen? "Aw yes! he is a manager isn't he!" Father Donnelly overheard the conversation and came over to assist Patricia, "Come now Patricia let's not bicker, it doesn't become you", Patricia shrugged Father Donnelly off, "I will have my say!". Jacqueline tried to comfort her, but she lashed out and caught the side of her face! Everyone was in shock, Father Donnelly steered Joan away. Dylan came to Jacqueline's rescue. "I am ok Dylan the poor woman is heartbroken with grief. Patricia and Lydia came over to Jacqueline and voiced their opinion; there was no need for her to strike you like that. Jacqueline made it clear that we all should make allowances at the sad time. They all hugged one another.

It was getting dark, and the paper lanterns shone like beacons in the water, even though it was a sad time the beacons seem to personify the joy of light, the joy of togetherness. The moon was out which hovered over those lost souls. The waves calming folded over and over gliding the paper lanterns higher and higher. As Jacqueline looked out in her garden, she could see the fourteen small specks of light as they floating away in distance like a dream subsiding was it my imagination? Jaqueline sat for a while in the garden and had a quiet talk to God. "Why was my Declan saved and not the others, why was that? she questioned, I am eternally grateful, but I am puzzled why this should be?". She sat and listened to see if she could fathom the likes of it? We can only help those in need she thought to herself as she watched the waves slither over the rocks...

Jacqueline sat back in her garden chair as she recalled the memories of her dear Mother and Father, Jacqueline got lost in the moment and went back in time remembering her father's passing and her mother's passing thereafter, it doesn't seem 15 years ago, how time flies. She thought about all those happy times at the beach. As tears trickled down her face Niamh came to sit by her. They hugged each other and Niamh changed the subject to poetry and literature as Niamh was very keen on getting to Dunston University which would only be 12 months away. She was always astute to her mother's feelings and knew how to cheer her mam up with poetry and literature, as always, a favourite with her mam. She hugged her Mam and said, "I am so glad mam that dad will be ok, and I am sorry for those who have lost their loved ones". I know hinny it's going to be a trying time for all concerned. We will get through this, we will. They made their way back into the house. Colm was in bed and Emily was sorting out her wool collection for next day at work. A sombre night it was…

Chapter 9

Jacqueline awoke early the next morning, and her thoughts were all over the place as she was trying to focus on the daily tasks, "Oh for goodness' sake", she said to herself, a good walk done the beach to her favourite cove to get my head straight as she was still talking to herself on her walk. It was a misty morning at first and the shimmering sun came glistening through, it's warmness seem to cascade over Jacqueline's shoulder. "Oh, I love the sea and sand it's a medicine no one can prescribe, as she muttered to herself. The alone time was always a great recipe to get your head straight and get on with the tasks ahead. Firstly, Jacqueline would head to hospital and hopefully get the news that Declan would be coming home soon as he was doing well. In the afternoon she would visit Patricia to offer her support. A good brisk walk along the beach and then she was set for the day's tasks ahead.

Mr Charleston the Surgeon had arrived at the hospital and was on his rounds, when he entered the room to see how Declan was doing, he found that Declan was responding to the medication with regards to his co-ordination and balance. It was now time for Declan to get to grips with walking around, the plan was for Declan to stay a few days to assess his walking abilities, it's just a precaution to make sure he is fully capacitated before leaving the hospital. Jacqueline was over the moon with that. She smiled at the Surgeon and he too reciprocated. They both shook hands and Mr Charleston walked down the corridor and muttered to himself, "what a lucky fellow you are Declan Gibson". He was referring to Jacqueline and her beautiful smile and gorgeous eyes. "Time to move on ", he said to himself.

Declan and Jacqueline warmly embraced each other. "It will be so wonderful to have you back my love", she said whilst brushing her hand against his cheek. Declan looked a little nervous as he was still feeling that little bit insecure which was unusual for him, but he was determined to get back to normal.

Dylan arrived to see how his brother was doing, he looked like he needed a bed beside Declan. Jacqueline looked up at Dylan and thought to herself it will be best to just leave the questions after the visit. Declan was getting a bit tired after his assessment so they both stayed a little while, but Jacqueline couldn't wait to have that chat with Dylan.

As Jacqueline and Dylan left the hospital, Jacqueline suggested they grabbed a coffee, and she guided him towards the small garden at the back of the hospital where there is a sitting area. Dylan looked awfully pale and hadn't shaven. "What is going on Dylan", Jacqueline asked. "I am all over the place Jacques, I thought I could just get over Serena, I just don't think it would work between us, we are from two separate worlds. Jacqueline looked outraged at that statement, "Oh don't be so ridiculous Dylan, we are not living in the dark ages now". Declan explained that it was her father that seems to be causing the rift between them, he was convinced of that. Jacqueline turned to Dylan and gave him some sound advice, she tells him to go home dust himself off and get himself back on track, firstly by looking after himself is a priority. His frame of mind was not on anything, so Dylan decided to push himself back into work and go out with the lads. Jacqueline was surprised she thought he would want to go and see Serena and sort things out. Dylan was not in that frame of mind at all. He was happy that Declan was on the mend and now he needed to mend himself.

Serena was so upset with Dylan as she herself thought he would come round. Serena's father had planned a dinner party that night and invited an associate of his Justin Aspley, a young and upcoming Solicitor who he thought would be a great person for Serena to get to know…. Serena was none the wiser that evening, but she did think it was rather odd that her father had asked her if she was dressing for dinner? Serena always changed for dinner after a day's work at the office. Serena was always impeccably dressed whichever the occasion. Serena wore her pale blue blouse with a frilly collar and cuffs and navy slacks and ballerina shoes she loved that relaxing look, with her hair tied back with a navy-blue scarf. As she entered the dining room the doorbell rang and she went straight to the front door, as she opened it a tall man with blonde hair, blue eyes, wearing a very expensive tweed jacket with cream shirt and fawn trousers. He spoke first with a posh London accent, "Hello you must be Serena, I have heard so much about you", he went on to say. Serena was taken back by the remark, "Sorry are you here to see my father?". "Well, yes and no", he quickly replied I am invited to dinner, I work alongside your father. As Serena escorted him to the dinning-room she gave her father a confusing look as she was wondering what was going on here ". As the conversation turned to riding, it turned out that Justin was a great rider and loved to get on his horse most weekends and sometimes evenings. He lived in the small rural village of Ramstone, he had small cottage with acres of land which was taken up by his stables. Ramstone was only 4 miles away from the Inskips. Serena's father was animated and was determined to get the conversation close to them both deciding to go riding together, well, it didn't take long as Serena had a great passion for riding and the two of them were getting on quite well. Serena's mother wasn't too convinced as she felt Justin was showing signs of being quite arrogant, she thought in her mind.

It was decided that Justin and Serena would go riding on that Saturday which was only two days away. Serena was now of the view, why not, Dylan isn't about to call he hasn't called for a few weeks now, he will be out with his friends, so I am doing what I love to do, she thought to herself. Her mind was still fuming over Dylan, and it wasn't going to simmer down just yet ...

Saturday arrived, Justin and Serena decided to meet up on the far field which was halfway between their two homes. Serena loved her horse, Greengage, he was beautiful black and white horse, and she declined to ride one of Justin's horses. Justin Horse was big black horse, named Boulter. They strolled along the countryside and then Justin decided to showboat a little by cantering over the hillside. Serena thought whatever you can do, I can do better. Serena showed him a thing a two that afternoon, Justin was getting quite taken with Serena, he was so particular and so precise in his manner; possessive by nature, as he had a past of being extremely possessive. The day ended on a surprising outlook as Serena had quite enjoyed herself. Justin decided to ask Serena out to dinner that night to end on a beautiful day of riding, Serena accepted, and he had provisionally already booked a table at the blue lakeside, as he was always so precise in his actions...

Mr Inksip Serena's father was elated his plan was going well. Charlotte, Serena's mother knew all too well that it was Serena's way of trying to get over Dylan, Justin was a rebound, and it wouldn't stay its course, Charlotte was confident of that as she knew her daughter, her feelings are bruised, but bruises get better she was convinced of that, her only worry would be that Justin may cause havoc among the family.

The table was booked for 8pm and there was a lovely pub on the riverside to go onto which had jazz music playing and Justin had decided that was what happening that night. Serena was happy to go along with it. It turned out not to be such a disaster as the food and music were very good. Justin was a good talker and loved talk about his attributes and accomplishments to try and impress Serena, she wasn't that convinced, although she thought his library of books were interesting as he loved to read about architecture and art. Serena loved Art, she was a great fan of the renaissance period of Art. Serena had decided to go on another date as she hadn't got any other dates lined up, as she was still in the back of her mind thinking about Dylan.

Dylan at this time was out with the lads, at the quayside, he joined in the karaoke, but he was drinking a little bit too much these days. Jacqueline had noticed that pale exterior of his and she pointed out to Dylan, "Drinking is not doing your looks any good Dylan, so you better pull yourself together, Declan is home on Monday, and I don't want to see you until you get your act together". Jaqueline was brutal with Dylan, and he was shocked to say the least, as Jacqueline had never been like that with him ever... he had never known Jaqueline to use that tone with him. He felt quite ashamed of himself, and it did the trick as Dylan decided to lay off the booze for a while and he did so, looking much better for it.

Monday had arrived and Declan was home he was looking that much better, it seemed months since he had been home, but it was only four weeks. Declan felt rather strange, but it was a nice strange he felt. He told Jacqueline he didn't want too much fuss and the family had decided to do everything as normal. They had dinner that night and Declan was happy in his favourite armchair, and he stayed up until 9pm that evening. They had enjoyed playing a little monopoly before bed. Declan was quite worn out by 9pm and his thoughts and flashbacks of the accident had started to comeback in the night as he woke up several times. His thoughts were on John and the others who had died... It was going to be a long haul before he was ever able to get back to normal. Jacqueline had heard him wake but she didn't want to get alarmed about it as the Surgeon had explained to her that these things will happen, and they will pass. Jacqueline knew in her mind that Declan wouldn't want her fussing over him, it was his way, no fuss. He was having the flashbacks and night terrors for several months and as the months went by Jacqueline knew in her mind Declan was strong enough to get through this and he did.

Patricia too was getting to grips with her loss, along with the other grieving wives, and the village was trying to put things behind them. The colliery had its final inspection, and the verdict was unexplained explosion as the fire dampers were not working and they were inspected a week before the explosion, so it was uncharacteristic for them not to working. It was concluded that it was unexplained. It would be a while longer before the colliery re-opened as further health and safety equipment were being installed.

There were mixed feelings in the village about the reopening of the mine, but most of the men wanted to get back to work and look after their family. It was understood at the final meeting on Wednesday that the colliery would be opening the following week as all checks would be updated within days. A big cheer went up at the community hall from all the working men, the women were a little subdued. Patricia did not attend.

Declan was invited to meet up with the Superintendent at the colliery to discuss his future. It was decided that Declan would take up an administration post in the office due to his head injury. Mr Charleston his surgeon advised strongly that Declan should take up such a position. Declan was reluctant at first, but he knew he would have to do this for his sake and for the sake of his family. He wasn't looking forward to it.

The day ended quietly as Declan sat in his favourite armchair feeling forlorn and for the first time in his life feeling unsure of his future, as Jacqueline entered the room she put her arm on Declan's shoulder and said, "If anyone can turn his hand to a different approach to their job, you can Declan Gibson, don't forget that, I am going up now". Declan kissed his wife goodnight and sat for some time and realised where his strength comes from his dear wife, who spurs him on to achieve almost anything. He was better now, still nervous but better. The lights went out and night came quickly...

Chapter 10

In the early hours of the morning Jacqueline suddenly awoke, brushed her eyes, and sat at the bottom of the bed, "Oh what a wonderful dream I was having, yes, "It's time to get the Book Club up and running again", as she smirks at herself through the dressing table mirror. I will start today and get all the group together for a coffee morning. It wasn't long before everyone was present at the Community Centre, they were all glad to go and have a good get together. It had been ages since they had done this. It was decided after some discussion, and plenty coffee and cake that everyone should take out some history books from the library on South Shields, and they would discuss the following week on the different aspects of history in the town. Hadrian Wall was a favourite amongst many, although it was across the river, it was a talking point. The older members in the group wanted to explore the old trams of transport in South Shields, and the how the beaches and promenades had changed. There is a lot of history in South Shields, Jacqueline went on to say. Everyone was elevated and thanked Jacqueline for getting them out of the doldrums. Patricia gave Jacqueline a surprising hug and thanked her for taking the grief away for a few hours at least. It was great gathering and coffee and cake to finish it off. Jaqueline was so pleased it went so well.

It was going to be a great day for Jacqueline, and she was hoping it was going to be the same for Declan as he headed out to his new position at the Shipyard, now to be in the office, as Assistant Office Manager; he was to report to the Office Manager and his duties would be on the statistics and estimating of materials for the colliery. He was to have 6-month training on this, he was rather nervous, but excited at trying something different. The office had several different alcoves and adjoining little steps up to them. Declan was in the far-left alcove which looked out at the sea which he was very happy with, a window with a view. As he glanced out to sea, he felt a rush of calm go through his bones, "Maybe it won't be so bad after all" …

There were 10 men in the office, aged between 25 years – 55years. They were a lively lot, but when the bell went heads down to work, break times 15 mins in morning and 15 mins afternoon. One hour lunch, it was so different for Declan as he just worked through and grabbed a bite as and when, he wasn't used with this. The office closed at 5.30pm which was another shock to Declan's system he was not used with such a routine. He was determined to give it his best shot.

Declan's first day was not as bad as he anticipated, as he was very good at adapting to new ideas. This new job title Statistician/Estimator he acquired was in fact quite interesting as he was familiar with figures, and drawings being a Manager at the Colliery. The Office Manager, Simon, believes Declan will be a great asset to the office.

As Declan arrived home Jacqueline was eager to find out how his day had gone. The family all sat down to tea. and after tea Declan talked about all the staff and his job description and those funny hours as he laughed. Jacqueline felt that he would a great turning point for her husband and a safer one. The children were so happy to see their father smiling so happily, Colm felt that it would be a good move for his dad. They were all very proud of him. It was decided they would all walk along the beach and grab an ice cream on the sea front as it was a lovely evening.

Jacqueline thoughts were engaged as well, as she was still beaming from her happy day of events at the Community Centre. As Declan turned to Jacqueline, "What are you smiling at then, grinning like a Chesire Cat". Jacqueline explained all to Declan about the Book Club gathering; they hugged and kissed each other as they went hand in hand and walked along the promenade. "I think I will pay our Dylan a visit later if that's ok pet ". Jacqueline responded with a smile, "Of course love he needs sorting out Declan". Declan smiled and knew Jacqueline was right about this. Declan arrived at Dylan's as he answered the door, he had a glass of whiskey in his hand. "Come in bro, join me". Declan declined. "What's the matter with you then, just have one at least ". Alright just the one, you know I don't drink much now since the accident. "Aw yes, sorry ", Dylan responded. What is going on Dylan lad, you cannot keep drinking like this you know. I thought you had laid off the source. I know, I am going to get myself together. Why don't we go down to the gym tomorrow night like we use to. Dylan was happy to accept, "I need to have a good work out", as Dylan glanced at Declan with a sorrowful look of his face, "It will do me good for sure". Declan gave Dylan a cheeky wink, "That's my bro".

The gym sessions were doing Dylan the power of good, as he was getting back to his usual self again. He was using every apparatus in the gym he could find available, whilst Declan would keep to his lightweight sessions and push Dylan along at the gym. It was great therapy for them both,

Saturday night had arrived, and Dylan was to meet up with the lads, he was not going to get smashed tonight. They started at Rigby's bar and Dylan was drinking half pint, the lads ribbed him for that, but he was not going to be deterred. As he made his way to the men's room, he caught a glimpse of Serena and Justin entering the bar, as he stood back, he overheard them talking about riding together the next day. Dylan was stunned he held back and didn't want them to see him, he left the bar and walked along the sea front and sat on a bench to gather his thoughts. Wow! What was that she didn't waste much time did she… he thought to himself. Riding indeed, ok, I can take riding lessons. What was he thinking, he wasn't really thinking but the idea of learning to ride a horse. The idea appealed to Dylan, "It will keep me fit in the process were his thoughts. The next day he called the riding school, and he joined up for a 3-month programme. It's done he said to himself, and he seemed elevated about the whole thing…

Dylan's lessons at first were rather ropey he was finding it rather tough, but he was encouraged by the instructor as he had the basics right at least and it will take a few weeks before he gets the hang of it. After four weeks everything was starting to come together, and he was decided that he would stay for the three months programme, he was thinking of pulling out after the first week, but persevered.

It was Dylan's last month of his training and the instructor advised Dylan that he could ride out on his own at the top field he was getting very good at riding now and there was no reason why he shouldn't have a good gallop on the top field.

As Dylan approached the top field, he was galloping along enjoying the ride when suddenly he caught a glimpse of two riders, he couldn't make them out just yet as they were quite far away, as they got nearer, he then realised it was Serena! Serena! Pulled up suddenly! Her face in shock! "What are you doing here riding Dylan? "I have been riding for some time actually, feeling very pleased with himself. Justin looked rather put out, "Shall we move on Serena", he said rather abruptly. Serena and Dylan gazed into each other's eyes what seemed to be an age, and that was why Justin was rather put out... as you can imagine dear reader this romance isn't going to go away for Serena and Dylan.

As Justin and Serena pulled into the stables, Justin turned to Serena, "Who the hell is that you were speaking to"? He is an old friend, old friend! Justin was furious, as he glared at Serena, "It looked more than that to me". Serena didn't like Justin's tone or manner; he was not gentleman like at all... false pretences she thought to herself. He comes across as a gentleman but is he really Serena thought to herself, was she was starting to see the real Justin?

Serena called it a day and Justin was getting rather possessive, he was very reluctant to call it a day. Serena pointed out that she was meeting up with the girls that night and Justin was not convinced. Eventually they parted ways that late afternoon, not before Justin found out where she was going that night.

As Serena arrived home, she looked in a daze a start of a trance, seeing Dylan again gave her goose bumps at the back of her neck, she knew she was still very much in love with Dylan.

Serena's father quizzed her about the day and Serena just brushed it off as a good day riding, her father seemed pleased with himself as the thought it was a great match Serena and Justin. Charlotte her mother knew there was something not right with the day's riding, she couldn't help noticing Serena's facial expression; a little frustration in her expression was there to see, but Mr Inskip was too engrossed with his matchmaking to notice.

Serena's friends had arrived at her home, and they were all going out in the minibus together. It was to be an exciting night as they were going to Newham town to a new club, 'The Vesta'. The minibus was full of laughter and noise and the bus driver couldn't help but laugh along with them. Jessica, Sandy, Nola, and Elise were all dressed up in their 60s dresses with high boots and ponytails. already for the big night. They thanked the bus driver and gave him a tip with this fare, he looked stunned for a moment and looked up to Jessica who was the noisy one, "You look after yourself and watch each other backs, have a good night". Jessica beamed at him, "Oh we will, we always look after each other", as they skipped and linked each other into queue, which was quite long to say the least, they didn't mind at all.

They had arrived, the crowds were now gathering it took them an hour to wait before they could get in. Justin jealously was getting the better of him, he drove to the club an hour before Serena arrived and entered the club in disguise, he wore a 60s cap and flares and even dyed his hair! So not to be recognised; he was menace! consumed with Serena, he had pictures copied and printed all over his bedroom. It seemed that Justin was portraying a character like that of a Jekyll and Hyde. Serena has no idea what she had gotten into with this man as he was very clever and hid all his compulsive characteristics. He acted completely normal in the workplace with gentleman like manners. Everyone thought very highly of him, especially Serena's father.

The night was going well, and the girls were having a great time and danced the night away, they all had admirers that night, including Serena. It was decided they would all leave together a except for Jessica who was asked out by an admirer she was beaming. Serena's spirits were lifted, for what are good friends for but to spend time with, as they all laughed and putting their arms around each other's shoulders. "We are the best of besties aren't we", Jessica was merrier than ever, always the joy of the party. "We are the besties".

As they left the club, Justin was not far behind them and followed Serena all the way home. He was completely obsessed. He had parked his car just on the lane near Serena's bedroom waiting impatiently for the light to come on, as he looked through his rear window, glaring with rage, not even aware of his image that of a deranged human being. He watched with bated breath as Serena entered the room and unfortunately for him, she had shut the curtains promptly. He slumped back in his car seat brushed his hair back and gave out a peculiar laugh as he admired himself in the mirror. He drove home at speed, and hurriedly entered the bathroom to wash out the dye in his hair and transformed himself back to usual self, whatever that maybe? He spent the rest of the night lusting over Serena's pictures. He would win her back with his softly manner. He knew Serena loved Orchids and that was the plan for the next week.

Chapter 11

It was Monday and Dylan couldn't stop thinking about Serena and their meeting, but it was the sight of Justin being with her that prevented him from calling her, he wasn't in the habit of bowing down to anyone, too proud for that. As he stood in the bathroom with a sulking look on this face. He was bruised, he looked in the mirror and stared at himself. "This won't get things done", he shook his head, and hurried along as work was in the midst and he was going to be late at this stage. He grabbed an apple and dashed to the car.

Dylan decided he would concentrate on work this week and not let any distractions get in his way. It was a busy week, as there was an unscheduled ship to come into dry dock, it was navy ship, so all hands-on deck if a navy ship came into dock unannounced. It certainly was a week of distractions when it came to work, as Dylan had his hands full, there were a lot of repairs to the ship, and it had to be ready to sail by Friday.

Friday arrived, and Dylan gave out a sigh of relief, as the ship was ready to sail, and it looked magnificent everyone was proud of their achievements on this one. A good, earned night out for the lads were on the cards. Dylan, however, was too tired for a big night as he had been working around the clock, he decided to have a quick drink with the lads and head home to his bed. His thoughts drifted towards Serena once again, he had decided not to call Serena, even though he had picked the telephone up numerous of times but didn't make the call.

As Dylan slowly walked to his front door and headed straight for the bedroom, he fell on top of his bed and lay there, "I know what I will do I will stroll down to the Brunch Bar tomorrow. As Dylan recalls when he first met Serena it was on a Saturday around 11.00am, what a great time we had that day. Let's hope the same table is available, wouldn't that be coincidence if Serena turned up, as he was aware that her hairdressers was just around the corner. His thought drifted towards their first meeting and his eyes became heavy, and eventually Dylan slipped into a deep sleep.

Saturday had arrived and Dylan walked into the Brunch Bar, he had managed to get the same table. Serena at this time was at the hairdressers just around the corner. As she left the hairdressers, she passed by the Brunch Bar, and it was having the same effect on her; "This is where Dylan and I had our first meeting", Serena signed and looked in, her face lit up! as she spotted Dylan in the window, she gasped! Oh! Shall I go in? as looked at him, she smiled to herself, and muttered, "oh! Look at his lovely face and dimpled chin...

Dylan got out of his seat as he saw Serena walking towards him, she looked amazing with her new hairdo, hair flowing off her shoulders. "Hi", they both said nervously. Dylan spoke quickly afterwards, "Are you having lunch? Please join me, as Dylan looked into Serena's eyes. "Yes, I was just popping in for some lunch". Dylan got out of his chair, "No point in us sitting separately, that would be silly", Serena smiled back at Dylan as he pulled a chair out for Serena. The waitress came across to them "What would you like?". They both said together, "We would like the mackerel, eggs, and toast please", as they both laughed together. "How have you been Dylan?", "Not too bad now Declan is back to normal, and things are going well at the shipyard for me now. I am now senior engineer." "Oh, congratulations Dylan I am so pleased for you" Serena replied. "How about you Serena, are you seeing someone?" Dylan looked on pensively, hoping Serena would say no, not really. Serena gathered her thoughts and spoke. "I have been dating, as you probably gathered when you saw me out riding, his name is Justin, my father introduced us; he works alongside my father, we are not an item; I have only been out with him a few times, He is ok sometimes", as she looked away, a long silence occurred. Serena moved her chair little towards Dylan as the chairs were miles apart, "How about you Dylan, have you been seeing anyone lately", Serena waited eagerly for Dylan's reply, hoping it was a good reply and he wasn't seeing anyone

65

else. "I have been too busy for that, just go out with the lads now and then to be honest, it suits me fine".

It was a tense meeting between the two of them, nonetheless they did connect once again, as they both left the brunch bar and politely said their goodbyes by saying, "See you around sometime", with a rather eager look on their faces. Serena got into her car and drove slowly around the sea front, just thinking about what just happened, where did we go wrong? Oh, never mind.

As she made her way home, she saw Justin's car and gave out a sigh... "Oh really! this is all I need today". Serena's mother greeted at her at the door with a gloomy expression on her face, "Justin is in the drawing room with a bouquet of Orchids", Serena smiled. Well, he has brought my favourite flower so I suppose I should be sociable at least. As their eyes met Serena thought why Dylan couldn't be standing here, she thought. Nevertheless, she decided to let Justin take her out for dinner that evening. Serena's father was pleased about the whole thing. Serena's mother had that reserved look on the face, hoping that Serena would have declined the offer, "Well, she is old enough to make her own mind up", as she looked up to her husband who had a wry smile on his face.

The evening started out at the Italian restaurant Ginelli's it was very nice, but Serena couldn't get her appetite together, Justin had noticed that. He was determined to win her over at any cost! He suggested that they have the best wine and Serena's was impressed with the Chardonnay he had chosen. As the dinner progressed Serena became rather tipsy. Serena realised she should have eaten more; her emotions were running high. Justin seemed to take advantage of the situation and as they walked towards the car, he became rather amorous, and a little aggressive when they got into the car, his hands were all over her, she was not impressed and started to push him away and then she slapped him hard. "Don't ever do that again to me, ever! I will call a taxi. He slumped in the car seat and couldn't believe his actions! He got out of the car very remorseful; I am so sorry Serena I don't know what came over me except I was overcome with your beauty, I am so sorry, please forgive me. I will not touch you again, please get into the car, I will drive you home. She accepted, he couldn't stop apologising all the way home and got rather emotional. Serena started to feel sorry for him at this moment. I forgive you Justin, let's forget about it now please. He wished her goodnight and asked politely if he could call her the next morning. Serena reluctantly agreed. Justin drove down the lane and gave out a loud peculiar laugh, checked his mirror at himself and said loudly! that's the way I will play it from now on...

Serena's mother Charlotte was getting increasingly worried about her, as she felt she was making a mistake going out with Justin. She couldn't put her finger on it, but she had that awful feeling there was something not right about him, he didn't sit well in her mind of thoughts.

It was getting late, and Serena was keen to get to her bed, she gave her mum a loving hug and walked wearily upstairs and fell into her bed with her inner thoughts of Dylan which were taking over her whole sense of being. Serena was convinced the romance between them was dwindling away… but the heart strings were still tucking away at her, and she couldn't get him out of her mind.

The next morning as promised Justin called, and Serena was too tired to say no to him and agreed to go out with him once again. Serena's father overheard the conversation and skipped into his study, as Charlotte looked on with a dismayed look, she waited until Serena had finished her call and approached her directly, "You don't have to go out with this man just because your father likes him Serena". Serena asked her mother why she didn't like him so much, "Just a feeling dear", she replied. Serena hadn't opened to her mother about Justin, which was uncharacteristic of her as she always told her mother everything. It is as if she had gone into some sort of daze with the loss of Dylan and seemed to not really get to grips with everything. She was however functioning well at work it was the only thing that was keeping her going.

Meanwhile, Justin was hopping with delight as he arrived at the office, and he had lunch with Serena's father and gave the indication that things were getting serious between himself and Serena. Serena's father looked a little surprised as he was an old-fashioned man with old fashioned ideals. He replied to Justin's remark by saying, "A good long courtship Justin it's the best way to go about it as it seals the commitment to one another, trust me as I am the experienced one here". Justin smiled at him in an awkward way and said, "Yes, you are probably right about that". He wanted Serena's father in his pocket. As he left him to go back to his office, he shut the door and slammed the filing cabinet with rage! this was not what he was wanting. He decided in his mind that he would guide Serena with his plan to get engaged before the summer was out which was only a few months away. Serena at this time in her life was just floating through life and it might not be that difficult. Justin was very astute and knew he had a soft caring beautiful woman whom he could manipulate.

Dylan at this time was determined to keep his riding lessons going, he was now really enjoying the prospect of riding each weekend. He was hoping to meet up with Serena again at the top field he thought, she must be there at least one Saturday.

As he finished work that day he decided to drop in and see Declan and Jacqueline and give them the news about his riding lessons. Declan was impressed and he was also impressed with Dylan's appearance, "The fresh air is doing you good bro", he said to him. "I am loving it bro", as Dylan grinned with his boyish looks.

Niamh and Colm entered the room, and Colm was interested in his riding lessons. "Can I come along to the stables Uncle Dylan, I would love to have a go at drawing some of the horses, something I have never really achieved. Dylan was delighted to take Colm along with him on Saturday next. Colm entered the conversation with Declan and Dylan as they were talking of how things were going for Dylan at the Shipyard since he had been promoted. Colm asked Dylan about his chances of getting an apprenticeship. Dylan replied, "Don't worry young un, I will sort that out for you". Colm beamed with excitement. Jacqueline approached Dylan, "Are you sure Dylan?" "Of course, I am, I am a Senior Engineer, I can pull a few strings for our young un here", as he smiled at Colm. Niamh winked at Colm and brushed his hair back! "Go get him our Colm". Colm retaliated and ruffled Niamh's hair, they wrestled for a moment, "Come on you two behave yourselves, stop that clowning around now, dinner is on the table", as Jacqueline started to bring in the evening meal for all. Roast Pork with roast potatoes, apple sauce and stuffing with plenty of vegetables. They all ate heartily and always enjoyed having Dylan at their table, he was forever the laugh and soul of a conversation, an interesting one at that. He was always goading Colm about his football technique and wind him up terribly. Declan always the referee between them, it ended well, Declan made sure of that. Dylan never missed a match his nephew was playing in.

As the night fell in, Declan and Jacqueline fell into each other in the bed and said, "We have all of children sorted for the future, how good is life for us they said to one another. Our Niamh will be at university in a few months, our Emily is thriving at the Wool Shop and now Colm. and you my love so back to normal and thriving in your job. "I am so proud of you my love", as Jacqueline turned to her husband. Lights were out for a loving evening...

Chapter 12

The day had arrived for Jacqueline to head to library to sort out the Book Club gathering, with an energetic smile on her face, "I hope everyone is in good spirits and had a good week reading". It was flaming June, and the temperatures were 25c. As Jacqueline walked along the sea front, she noticed how crowded the beach was, and the donkey rides were going well. The Shuggy boats were filling up with children queuing for hours. The fish bar was full to the brim. Everyone had their deck chairs out and the lifeguards were busy on the lookout to make sure everyone was safe in the water. All the families with their hampers full of food and drink to avoid the queues at the fish bars and other restaurants.

Jacqueline got all the women from the book club, including Patricia and Joan. Come on girls she said let's get ourselves onto our lovely beach and find a quiet spot and we can all chat about our findings we have discovered about the history of South Shields. Everyone agreed, they all got together a picnic basket with towels to sit on, some brought deck chairs. Eventually they found a quiet spot just above the cove near Trow Rocks, which was hidden way, it was Jacqueline's favourite spot where she did all her thinking and writing her poetry. It was an ideal spot for them all to get together.

Patricia was elevated about her findings of the 18th century period, in particular, the smugglers that used to come ashore with contraband goods, such as whiskey, and cigarettes. As they arrived on land, they would be interrupted by the thieving gangs, it was a thriving time for the sailors. Not to mention the fisherman and their wives who made a tidy profit from the smuggling trade.

Joan had gone back in time to 9th century when the Vikings came ashore. Joan was interested in the earlier days. They raided the established settlements and controlled most of Northern

England. The conversation diverted to the Roman Fort, which was built in C1249D, a very big talking point even today as the Fort was still standing. As the conversation continued it was mentioned that the Shipyards and Mining community in 19 Century seem to be booming at the time. The Industrial period they called it that transformed the area. Everyone was engrossed in the history of Hadrian's Wall, built c.122AD. it's about 73 miles long, and still today it is an iconic sight. They had all forgotten how hot it was, and their faces were all burning. It was time to pack up and head home in the shade.

Jacqueline made her way back to the cottage; she was quite sun burnt on her arms and neck. Oh, what a lovely afternoon she thought, she was so pleased with Joan and Patricia who are now finding their way back to normality. "To read to know we are not alone". Jacqueline said to herself, she remembered her dear mother used to say that to her. I believe it was CS Lewis who said that she muttered to herself and smiled as she made her way to the kitchen. Time to get the tea on as the children were upstairs studying and Emily had arrived home from the wool shop and Declan will be home in half an hour. Lovely salad with new potatoes I think for tea today as it is so hot. She had all the windows open, as she looked out of her kitchen window the sky was so blue and the reflection seem to filter along the waves, what a breath-taking sight. The Beach was at its best today.

Niamh came downstairs, she walked up and down the kitchen trying to get up the courage to tell her mother that she wanted to live in at the Halls when she started University in September. All Niamh's friends were staying in the halls. Jacqueline turned around and said, "What's all this pacing about for young lady, got something on your mind?". "Yes, mam, please sit-down mam". This sounds ominous Jacqueline thought to herself. Mam, I want to live in at the halls as Kate and Jessica are living in, please say it will be ok for me to do this, as Niamh crossed her fingers. Jacqueline was stunned, we will talk about it when dad gets home, just as Jacqueline had said this, Declan walked through the door. Dad! Niamh said as he came through the door. "What! is the house on fire or something?", as Declan look puzzled? Jacqueline looked at Declan and they all sat round the kitchen table. Niamh put her case across, and Declan spoke first and said, "I think it's good idea as you will be with your friends but mind your home at the weekend". "I will Dad, I will!" Niamh shrieked with delight. Jacqueline wasn't that keen as they were both close and it left this ache in her stomach, as if she was losing Niamh for good. Emily will be pleased Niamh thought as she would have a whole room to herself at least for 5 days anyway. Oh, the house was full of excitement and Colm joined in too, for he thought it was great idea for Niamh to spread her wings. Everyone was elated except for Jacqueline. Declan took her aside after tea and they both took a walk along the beach to air things out. Jacqueline had her say by pointing out this will be the first time Niamh has been away for more than one night and I am worried with all those students and no parenting. Declan reassured Jacqueline by saying they have housekeepers you know. "How do you know Declan?" Jacqueline asked. Don't you remember Tom's lad went to university he used to tell us all about it down the pit as he was so proud. They have support groups, and the University is well managed. Jacqueline looked amazed, "I had no idea" she said.

They took a long stroll along the beach as the waves were sultry and slow and glimmering away and the calmness of the walk made Jacqueline feel slightly at ease with it. Declan knew how close they were, and it would be a big wrench at the beginning for Jacqueline, but he knew she would eventually get use with it.

As they arrived back at the cottage, Aileen and Arthur had arrived for a visit, as they had been for a car drive and thought to just drop in for a cuppa. Jacqueline was pleased to see her sister and they chatted for hours, mainly about how the wool shop was doing and about the new expansion next door, and of course Niamh's news. Aileen didn't know how to console Jacqueline as she hadn't had any children and didn't really know how she would feel if one of her children were to leave home. She instead changed the subject on to the book club as she knew how Jacqueline thrived on this.

The telephone rang and Sara, the youngest of the sisters, who called she was asking Jacqueline if it would be ok for her to come and visit. Jacqueline was elated, as was Aileen. Sara would stay in their beach house along the coast, as it was vacated, Jacqueline had not rented it out this year. Aileen pensively looked on, "Why she was coming on her own? she thought. Sara was to arrive that very weekend and Jacqueline and Aileen were so happy they were seeing their baby sister as they never had many get togethers.

The weekend was upon us, and Jacqueline did a quick clean at the Beach house for Sara's arrival. Aileen was coming along later. It was 1pm and Jacqueline made her way back to the cottage in time for Sara's arrival. Just has she set foot in the door; a taxi arrived with Sara in it. They both greeted each other with a tight hug and kiss. As they sat around the table Jacqueline noticed how much weight Sara had lost and how pale she looked. Sara just spurted it out, "John has left me for a young woman!". Jacqueline looked shocked never in this world would she think that John would leave Sara. Sara was lighter haired than Jacqueline and was always thought of in the family as the best looker and had the best figure.

Sara told the whole story about John being late from work every night, he was in the wholesale business and sold goods to all the retail shops. His excuse was the orders were piling up. Sara decided to check up on John and she caught him leaving work with a blonde lady as he was holding her hand and kissing her. She looked 10 years younger than him. It all came to a head the other evening when I told him I knew. He begged me not to leave and said it was all over, but I couldn't stay Jacqueline, I just couldn't the betrayal was too much.

Jacqueline decided to get out the Chardonnay as she knew Sara loved Chardonnay. They ended up getting rather tipsy and laughing about it, Jacqueline saying to Sara, "I think poor John must have had a mid-life crisis, perhaps men have the change of life". They both laughed and then Sara began to cry and said,

"The sad thing is I still love him so much". Jacqueline pointed out that she should stay for at least a month and let John sweat it out.

The next day, Jacqueline changed all her schedule for the whole week to spend entirely with Sara, they visited museums and art galleries, as Sara loved to visit the museums. They ventured over to Holy Island to take in the atmosphere and the spiritual connection. They managed to get through lots of coastlines along Northumberland that week for the views and art and craft facilities were plenty.

As the week came to an end, John had telephoned repeatedly all week and then he turned up on the last day of their adventures as they both were walking to the beach house John stood outside the door. Jacqueline turned to Sara and said, "I will leave you alone, just come up to the cottage when you are ready". Sara turned to John and they both went inside. John looked terrible he hadn't slept all week. Sara sat down and pointed out to John that she couldn't come back straightaway, she needed time, she wasn't say no to him, but she wasn't ready to go back just yet. She asked him to respect her privacy for a bit longer and she would call him in a few weeks' time. John was relieved a little as there was hope and he could see from Sara's eyes, there was hope.

They walked along the beach and talked some more, John explained that he was not in his right mind going with a younger woman. He wasn't all to blame as Anne the young lady was promiscuous. He was taken in by her allurement. "I am so ashamed of myself Sara", he said. Sara believed him, but the hurt was too raw and she was sticking to her guns and would see him in a few weeks. Sara said goodbye to John and made her way to the cottage.

Jacqueline was so proud of her sister, and they all sat round for tea. Declan put the radiogram on and played all of Stevie Wonder hits as he knew Sara was a big fan. They danced the night, and it was if Sara had forgotten about her hurt for a little while anyway...

Chapter 13

It was dull misty Sunday morning and Sara decided to go to Mass with Jacqueline, Sara wasn't a regular, but she did go for the big feast days, Christmas, and Easter. Father Donnelly was in high spirits as usual. He service was always very lively, no matter what the weather. Sara was taken with such an energetic service, and she thanked Jacqueline was taking her along as she was reluctant at first.

Dylan was coming today for Sunday lunch and Sara got up to speed with Dylan's predicament with regards to Serena. Sara hadn't been acquainted with Dylan that much, but she could see the lad was suffering. Sara suggested that he should be bolder and telephone Serena and to meet up for coffee, "Just do it Dylan, it will put your mind at ease", as Sara approached him. He was on the verge on doing so, and he had decided he would do just that after a hearty lunch at the Gibson's.

Dylan arrived back at his apartment and telephoned Serena, it was lucky that Serena's mother had answered the telephone and Serena came to the telephone so surprised but happy; they both decided to go out that night for a drink. Serena kept this from her father and Justin as she didn't want any drama. Afterall, she didn't know the outcome of the tonight, it was only a drink, as she sighed with a disappointing look on her face.

Justin telephoned just before she was leaving the house and was very put out that she was going out, and asked who she was going out with. Serena hadn't really lied as she said it was friends, as Dylan was only a friend, wasn't he? She thought to herself…

As Justin paced up and down in his living room like a deranged animal, screaming at himself! "She cannot do this to me, who is she with, where has she gone? He was obsessed … He got into his sports car and drove incessantly around and around until he ran out of petrol! Outraged, he remembered he did have can of petrol in his boot for emergencies. "She must be somewhere, he decided to try every pub and every restaurant. He recalled Serena loved that little bistro in Durham, as he approached the car park, he could see them both as he had parked near the entrance. He sat in his car his eyes full of anger and jealousy. He was not going to approach them. "I am a Solicitor, a gentleman", he said to himself. Underneath his exterior wore a dark side of his nature that he couldn't control at times, but tonight and just tonight he would compose himself.

Serena looked stunning as usual, and Dylan dressed up for the occasion as usual for Serena. They were not short on conversation, and it was if they had never been away from each other. The chemistry was coming back in floods. Serena was surprised by his riding skills, and they had decided to go out riding, but she didn't want to go to the same riding school as Justin. There was another just outside of Durham, so they decided to meet up there that following Saturday afternoon.

Their lovely night together came to an end and Declan drove Serena home; it was past mid-night. Serena's parent had gone to bed and Serena was relieved about that. They kissed passionately and the attraction between them was imminent. Dylan left her walking into the house and thought to himself she is the woman I am going to marry. Serena turned and thought to herself as she gave him a wave, and whispered to herself, 'I love you '. Serena knew what she had to do, and she would do it. She was not going to go out with Justin again, she would need to let him down gently she knew that...

The next day Justin telephoned Serena he was very agitated when Serena's mother answered the telephone, Justin in fact was rather rude to Charlotte (Serena's mother). Charlotte stayed calm and composed and answered Justin with a cool voice, "Justin you seem rather abrupt, are you feeling well? as I said Serena is in the bathroom and I will let her know that you called". Justin composed himself as he always did, "I sincerely apologise Mrs Inskip for my abrupt manner, I am running late and just wanted a quick word with Serena before I head out", "Not to worry Justin", Charlotte replied, I will let Serena know and she will call you back I am sure when she is able. The telephone clicked off rather sharply from Justin's end, he was furious, his obsession with Serena was getting rather frantic.

As Serena came down the stairs, her mother called her into the drawing room. Serena, I have just taken a call from Justin, and I have to say that man is rather rude. Serena looked at her mother and grabbed her hand, "Mother I don't want to see him again, I think you're right about him he is too volatile, his mood swings are started to show when I last saw him". "Why did you not tell me Serena" her mother asked. "I was wanting to sort this out myself as I thought I may have overreacted". "Does this have anything to do with Dylan I wonder", Charlotte looked over with a smile on her face. Serena smiled back, "You are telepathic mother, I always knew you were". They both hugged and smiled with joy. The joy Serena was feeling now wasn't going to last, and there was Justin to contend with.

Serena left the house thinking of a perfect way to let Justin down, as she was walking towards her car, she could hear a car coming at some speed down the driveway and it was Justin! Serena was stunned by his urgency. He got out of the car and urged Serena to enter his car as he was wanting to have a private word with her. She got into his car, and he drove away, "What are you doing Justin, I have to get to work!" Justin was frantic! He wouldn't slow down! "You have been avoiding me, I saw you with Dylan". "What! have you been following me? Serena was shaking and trying to get a sentence together, she was scared! Justin blurted out, "You belong to me and no one else". As Serena tried to get out of the car, the car collided with another car and spun off the road. Serena hit her head against the dashboard, her hand protected her from the brunt of the steering wheel. Justin was quite unscathed just shook up from the impact.

A car driving past, pulled up to help the injured. Justin tried to grab Serena, but she pulled away and opened the car door, as she did so, a man put his hand out to ask if she was alright, he then went over to the driver's side and asked Justin if he was alright. He was just about to go the telephone box up the road when Serena shouted, "I will come with you!". "You shouldn't you have a gash on your head" he said. "Oh, that's just a scratch", she replied and followed him to the telephone box. At this time Justin just sat in his car, shocked and stunned and angry with himself for getting out of control of the situation.

The police and ambulance arrived, there were no fatalities from either of the cars, thankfully. Justin was keen to compensate the other driver, as he didn't want an investigation and the other driver was happy with the large compensation offer from Justin. The Police took statements from everyone, and Justin's statement was that of his brake's pads need replacing. Serena at this point was reluctant to say anything to the contrary, as she was too scared to say anything else. It was as if she was in shock and the paramedic was insistent, Serena had to be checked out at the hospital for concussion. Serena's mother and father were notified, and they would meet her at the hospital. Justin was checked over by the paramedic and he was fine. The paramedic remarked on how lucky they all were that no one was seriously hurt.

Serena was checked out by the Doctors and given a clean bill of health. Serena left the hospital with her mother and father. At this point Serena was reluctant to say anything until she got home. They all sat in the drawing room and Serena began to tell the whole story. Serena's father was so shocked he couldn't take it in, "I thought he was a gentleman, this won't do, it will not do!" he shouted. I will have a word with the partners at work, but I don't want him working in my firm. Serena's father was the major holder of, Inskip, Barrett and Walistone Solicitors, Commissioner of Oaths. Mr Inskip left his wife and daughter together as he headed to the office. At this time Justin was waiting for his car to be towed and a replacement car to get him to work as he was not going to miss a day's work he thought.

Mr Inskip and his partners agreed they would terminate Justin's employment; it was imminent with immediate effect.

Justin managed to get a replacement car and entered the office as if the morning events had never taken place.

Samantha his secretary informed Justin that he was to go to the boardman immediately. Justin was bemused, he had delusions of grandeur, "Maybe I am being promoted", smirking as he strolled along the corridor. As he entered the boardroom, it was made clear to Justin that his employment was ceased and he was to clear his desk, and a fellow colleague will ensure that he does not take any files away with him or client's telephone numbers. Justin implored the board to change their minds, as he put it was a misunderstanding between Serena and himself. He tried to say that Serena wasn't telling the truth and she fabricated some of her accusations. He stood up and said, "I am an excellent Solicitor and I have given my all to this firm and made you lots of money in the process". The board acknowledged the fact and generously gave Justin 3 months' notice with full pay of which it stipulates that he does not work the 3 months, he leaves today. Justin was escorted to his desk, and he left forthwith, as he got into his car, he muttered angrily to himself, "Serena is not getting away with this, it is not over by a long chalk" ….

Dylan arrived at Serena's, Mr Inskip was very polite with Dylan on this occasion, they both shook hand in a friendly manner. Serena's parents left the house to leave Dylan and Serena to their own devices. There was a casserole in the oven, so everything was set for them to have dinner alone. Serena's face was bruised but she covered it quite well with her make-up, or so she thought, Dylan noticed the swelling and couldn't compose himself. "Serena! What really happened in that Car". Serena put her arms around Dylan and said, "Let's just have dinner and some lovely Chardonnay first".

As they sat through dinner gazing at each other and trying to make small talk which wasn't going that well. Dylan was trying to eat faster so he could get to the bottom of what really happened. Dinner was finally over, and they sat in the drawing-room, it was calm room with a beautiful fireplace, with a cosy sofa to match.

Serena began to unfold that awful day when Justin drove off, "He wasn't supposed to be here", I was getting into the car to have a quick chat. Justin got aggressive and I kept asking him to turn around, he just kept repeating over and over, "You belong to me". I don't think he was going to take me back; I think he was abducting me to be honest. Dylan told Serena to go back to the Police and report this. Serena was of the view that her father had now dismissed him from work, and he would move on, and she wouldn't see him again. Justin is a clever man, and it would be my word against his she told Dylan. They cuddled into each other, and Serena went onto to say, Justin is gone now and to be honest I want to put all this behind us. They lay together for hours listening to soul music and a little classical as Serena loved Beethoven, moonlight serenade. Dylan mentioned how her father had greeted him in such a friendly way. Serena responded by saying, "My father has had his eyes opened over Justin, he now realises that class and money do not always mix with good manners and a good disposition. Dylan was happy with that response and they both realised how much in love they were on this night. Dylan did keep his composure and left at 11pm like a gentleman as the Inskips arrived back home. It was a lovely night all round for Dylan and Serena. Charlotte was happy that her husband had now seen sense where Dylan was concerned.

Meanwhile, Justin was back at his house, telephoning Serena, but when he dialled the number, it said "This number is no longer available". The Inskips had their number changed immediately after that awful day. Justin went into a frenzied fit, smashing the telephone at the wall. I will call her at work, I will get to her one way or the other he said to himself…

Chapter 14

Serena was full of energy on this bright and sunny day as she skipped her way to her car, it was going to be a busy day at the office as Serena was attending a Case Conference, a personal injury claim had to be sorted with the Barrister as the case was going to Court. She was upbeat as she knew her client had a good case, and they would win it.

As she arrived back at the office at noon there were 6 messages from Justin asking her to call him to talk. Serena tore them up and put them in the bin, she told her secretary Joanne to say that she is not available if he calls again. This went on all week and Serena was getting concerned now as she knew Justin would not stop this harassment.

It was time to go and have a word with dad as she entered her father's office with a concerned look on her face. Mr Inskip instructed that all calls from Justin to be diverted to his telephone, he will be deal with him directly. That very afternoon he called again, and Mr Inksip made it quite clear that if he calls again, he will be calling the Police and have him arrested. Justin responded by saying I am doing nothing illegal; I am simply just wanting to talk to Serena. Mr Inksip went on to further to say that he has friends in high places, and he will be arrested if he keeps telephoning. The telephone went down with a big bang! Justin had decided to take the matter further. He would be watching and waiting for his moment to get to Serena....

Mr Inskip telephoned his dear friend an Inspector at the local Constabulary Mr Steele. It was agreed that they would be surveillance on Justin, they have his car registration and his home address. Mr Steele told Mr Inskip to leave it to him, and he will keep him informed of any developments.

Mr Steele recruited a bright young Detective Constable Simon Jessop to do some digging into Justin's past. Simon was great at researching profiles. A very enthusiastic young man wanting to solve this problem. He came about that Justin had moved around quite a lot and he was born in Wiltshire in Marlborough. When Justin left Oxon University, he moved to Portsmouth to take up a position as an Article Clerk at firm of Solicitors Bryan and Steadman Commissioners of Oath, as he had failed his Solicitors final. Justin was a ruthless human being who ventured through law with a type of plagiarism no one seem to double check his credentials through his career, whenever anyone got close to him, he would move to another firm.

The young Detective came back to Inspector Steele with his recent finding; it turned out that Justin had worked for 6 firms before securing a contract with Mr Inskip's firm. Justin always managed to get great references to uphold his deceit. The inspector was very pleased with Simon's progress so far and said it's time to get into his personal life at all these firms. As the Inspector smiled at the enthusiastic young Detective he said, "Keep up the good work young man, and keep me posted ".

The search into Justin's private life took the young DC Jessop to Wiltshire, Oxon, Portsmouth, Westcliffe, Somerset, Dorset, and Gloucestershire and Cornwall. After further discussions with the Inspector, it was decided that the young Detective would need an experienced hand to guide him on this case as it is turning out to be more complexed than they thought. Detective Sergeant Russell Gable was to collaborate with all the police forces in that area to see if there had been any such reports of a Justin Aspley behaving irrationally or in fact more serious reports.

Russell and Simon were working well together, Detective Sergeant Russell was not shy of hard work and knew there would be a lot of files to go through, as some of the systems in the police force were not that user friendly with their filing systems. Detective Constable Jessop was only too happy to get stuck into the files.

After 3 weeks of delving and pursuing every avenue, it turned out that Justin Aspley had been accused of harassment and stalking 3 young ladies in his past, but no charges were brought against him as there was not sufficient evidence. Inspector Steele was of the view that this time he will not get away with it. DS Gable and DC Jessop will be on surveillance from now on.

Inspector Steele notified Mr Inskip and implored Serena to be very vigilant, and not at any time be left on her own indoors or outdoors. Serena was not fazed by all of this, after all she was of strong character and suggested wouldn't it be better if I coax him, and you could catch him in the act. Inspector Steele was not in favour of this, as in his experience when someone is irrational and possessive things could go wrong. Mr Inskip was also not in favour of Serena's bold suggestion. It was settled and the police will deal with this matter....

Dinner was at Inskips, and Mr Inskip was happy to have Dylan at this table and he apologised to Dylan after dinner by saying, "I made a mistake thinking you were not good enough for my Serena and I sincerely hope you will accept my apology". Dylan was taken back by this great gesture and eagerly accepted his apology. Charlotte was so pleased that her husband had now seen sense regarding Dylan, as Charlotte was beginning to like Dylan more and more and felt that he would make the ideal Son-in-law.

Mr Inskip and Dylan had a quiet moment; a man-to-man chat, as Mr Inskip was eager to fill Dylan with the full story of Justin Aspley as he knew Serena would play it down. They both decided to keep a close eye on Serena. "Call me Jonathan, Dylan", he replied, "I think we can dispense with the formalities, don't you?". Dylan was most surprised indeed, he thought Mr Inskip would never warm to him in that degree, "Wonders will never cease", as he smiled to himself...

In the meantime, the two Detectives spot Justin driving towards the Inskip home where he parked nearby. Justin was banging on the steering wheel as he spots Dylan's car. He eventually speeds off and the two Detectives pull him up for speeding; they get a good look at him and only give him a caution this time. Justin stared at the Detectives with his very apologetic stance; he looked rather calm and collective; Justin could always turn on the charm when it was needed the most. As the Detectives got into their car, they both said at the same time, "What a sleaze, clever with it". They were in the mood to arrest him there and then, but caution prevailed as Inspector Steele gave orders to watch and wait, they needed to catch him in the act to get a solid conviction... As the Detective turned to the young constable he made a point of saying, "We need to keep a very close eye on this guy, let's not lose our focus on this one lad". The young Constable was only too keen to oblige the Detective.

As Justin arrives back at this home, he starts to develop a plan to get Serena away from everyone. He had no idea the police were following his every move. His plan was to send flowers to Serena but sign the Card Dylan," meet me for lunch today at Rico's". Justin knew she would be there!

Serena left the office excited to see Dylan as she thought. The two Detectives followed Justin to the restaurant. DC Jessop eagerly spots Serena pulling up in her car, he turns to DS Gable, "What is she doing here?" They both decided to go into the restaurant discretely, as they approached the manager and explained the situation. DC Jessop sat opposite the table and DS Gable sat behind them. Serena looked shocked! Entering the restaurant as she spots Justin, she knew then the flowers were sent by Justin! Serena decided to play his game and smiled with a fake smile and said, Hello Justin what are you doing here? "I would have thought that it is obvious, I am madly in love with you, and you are with me, or you were with me". Serena pointed out to him that she had never said she was in love with him, "We only met a few times and went riding Justin", she said looking firmly at him and saying, "This has got to stop". Justin grabbed her wrist aggressively, "It will stop when I say it will stop". "I am leaving now, let go of my hand". Serena got up and as she turned, he grabbed her. DS Gable stood up and went towards Justin and said, "You let go of that young lady now". Justin lost it and aggressively punched the DS causing him to lose his balance. As DC Jessop approached with his handcuffs, "I am arresting you for assaulting a police officer". The young Constable read him his rights as he was taught in the Police Academy. Justin was even more furious and as DS Gable got up from the floor the Detectives ushered him away. Serena was shaken but so relieved that the incident was all over, as Justin will go to prison for assaulting a Police Officer.

DS Gable and DC Jessop arrived back at the Police Station and Justin was safely in the cell. Inspector Steele looked across at the DS and said, "That's going to be a shiner, better get some steak on that eye lad – well done you two". DS Gable turned to DC Jessop , "Got that wrong, should have let you sit behind him", as they both laughed.

Serena went back to work to catch up with her father and give him the full story of the day's event. Mr Inskip put his arm around his daughter and said, "How could I have got it so wrong, he seemed so articulate and charming and very precise with his workload?". Serena responded by saying, "Yes, father, he was a real-life conman and very good at it too, we have both learned a great deal from this father – back to work I think father as she kissed him on the cheek.

Serena walked down the corridor to her office she was happy now that she had her independence back, and she could get back to normal. On reflection, Serena started to the feel effects of the day's events, "I shouldn't have been so bold, I shouldn't have been so courageous, what was I thinking, or was the thought just to get that man out of my hair", as she sat down Serena started to shake somewhat, "It's just the shock, it will pass, I think I will have a tea with sugar, not normally a sugar person but I think today I will make an exception". Serena sat for some time and the tea and sugar seem to be so calming, she started to relax a little, until her next client, she looked into the mirror tidied her hair and make-up and patted herself on the thigh, she was ready for the rest of the day.

Chapter 15

Dylan decided to take Serena down to the Beach for a happy distraction from her ordeal with Justin and there was nowhere better that Sandhaven Beach. They arrived at the beachy head with the glorious stepping stones that lead to a lovely patch of sandy beach, it was Dylan's favourite as it is a secluded part of the beach. As Serena took the steps, there were so many, but it was beautiful journey to get to the bottom of them, Serena couldn't help but take in the breath-taking view, you can see sand and sea for miles, and the lighthouse looked so far away in the distance. Trow Rocks valiantly glowing in the sea, as the waves seem to cuddle around the edges of the rocks. She felt like she was on top of the world. Dylan packed a lunch and even brought the towels with him so they could take a dip in the sea. It was day of adventure, and Dylan was determined to give Serena the best day.

They found a lovely spot under a rocky alcove, and lay side by side just taking the sunshine and listening to the folding waves lash away. They could hear the surfers in the background getting ready to go into the water. "Time for lunch my love, I have packed your favourite Salmon and Cucumber sandwiches, Serena beamed with joy. Later, we can have a dip in the sea if you have a mind to. Serena Kissed Dylan gently and said, "I do have mind to".

Once the Surfers had gone further down the beach, Dylan grabbed Serena's hand and ran into the water, "Wait a minute Dylan, I need to tuck my dress up, Serena tucked her dress into her pants, Dylan looked on so surprised so surprised indeed! Serena was liberated she was jumping up and down in the water, Dylan in turned rolled his trousers up and they splashed about in the water what seem to be hours, they dropped heavily down in the sand soaking wet, but happy wet. They both ventured back to their little picnic in the enclosed alcove and dried off. Dylan turned to Serena and looked remorseful as he began to say, "I wish I hadn't turned you away, as I think you wouldn't have gone out with that Justin, and you would not have been part of such a terrible ordeal! Please forgive me for that my love". Serena put her arms around Dylan, "It's not your fault, right, it's not your fault, you had so much to contend with, your brother was your priority at the time, not me, I admire and respect you for that Dylan, there is nothing to forgive". Dylan kissed Serena passionately on the lips, "I love you so much". Serena gave Dylan a loving smile, and said, "I love you too". They lay there for seemed an age, just embraced in each other's arms.

Dylan had called on Declan earlier and it was all arranged that Dylan and Serena would be having dinner at the Gibson's. Serena was more than happy to go along with Dylan's plans. Sara arrived with news of her own, her husband John, he had rented a Beach House not far from the Gibson's Beach House. John was determined to get things back on track with Sara and he was willing to go the extra mile to do so. He was arriving that very weekend. Sara was apprehensive, but also pleased that John was making such an effort. It was a night full of conversation from all parties. Sara had noticed how Jacqueline seemed to be far away in all the conversations but decided to dismiss it as the conversation turned to Dylan and Serena, Dylan was quickly changed the conversation to music and that always got Declan on his feet. Everyone sat around listening to the sounds of the 60s.

Jacqueline was pre-occupied with Niamh's departure to university in the coming weeks as Niamh wanted to go early to get settled in her new surroundings at Dunston Hall. Niamh was so excited as her best friend Kate was also going to be there. Emily was happy for Niamh but would miss her a lot as they had shared a bedroom for so long. Colm was his usual self, laid back and not really bothered about it; a typical lad. This would be the first time Niamh had been away from home for a good while, but it was agreed she would be back during the holidays. Jacqueline, Declan, and Niamh sat out in the garden watching the surfers on the beach as it was the day for surfing as the wind was in a good place for the surfers to have a good glide across the waves. Niamh pointed out to her parents that she was a sensible teenager, and they should trust her decision to go and live in at university. Declan smiled at Niamh and said, "We do trust you, it just that we are trying to get used with the idea that you won't be at home for a good while". Niamh laughed aloud and said, "I am not going that far Dad! it's only 8 miles away". Jacqueline hadn't realised it was not that far, and hugged Niamh.

Sara joined them in the garden, and they all had tea and biscuits and enjoyed the lovely sunshine, whilst Niamh was so excited and would not stop talking about her modules at university. Firstly, she will study Jane Austen, Charles Dickens and the Brontës. They all listened to Niamh with great hopes for her.

Jacqueline had prepared a large buffet as Sara and John were also coming to dinner, Aileen and Arthur were also invited; a hot and cold buffet so everyone could choose whatever they liked, strawberries and cream or Jacqueline's famous Apple Pie for dessert. It was a warm evening Declan suggested that they should set up the outside tables with the gingham tablecloths. Everything was ready for 7pm.

Niamh, Emily, and Colm were too busy playing volleyball on the beach and didn't hear their father shouting for them to come in and get cleaned up. Jacqueline said, "Just leave them for now, they are enjoying themselves, it's such a lovely night, they will get hungry soon, mark my words as she smiled at Declan".

Dylan and Serena arrived first, followed by Sara and John. Declan introduced John to everyone, and they all commented on Jacqueline's lovely display of food and drink, John was the first to speak by saying, "Wow, I feel like I have just walked into a banquet, it is magnificent Jacqueline". They followed suit by congratulating Jacqueline on a fabulous spread of food. Jacqueline pointed out that it is just good old fashioned homemade food.

Emily, Niamh, and Colm could smell the glorious food and were quick to abandon the volleyball and quickly get changed to enjoy the lovely food. Emily was pleased Aileen was coming to dinner as she wanted to talk to her about a new window display at the wool shop, Emily was becoming quite creative in her job at the wool shop. Aileen was beginning to think that she should just hand everything over to Emily to sort out. Emily was elated. Colm was keen to chat with Dylan further about his apprenticeship. Dylan soon put his mind at rest about what to expect on the first week or so, Colm will be shadowing Dylan for the first week on the ship to get him used with the materials and the machinery. Dylan pointed out to Colm that he will only be doing manual work at first and will be trained properly on the machinery. The first week will be a good insight into how things operate around the ship.

Serena began to tell the full story to Jacqueline about the silly argument she had with Dylan at long time ago and she made a big mistake by going out with Justin, Serena poured her heart out to Jacqueline as they sat in the kitchen pouring coffee out for everyone. Jacqueline was stunned, but very happy that she had made up with Dylan and pointed out that she felt that they made a great couple and were well suited to each other. Serena was so surprised with herself as he had never poured her heart out like this, not even to her own mother. They both laughed at each other as they realised, they had been talking for so long and the coffees were stone cold… "We best make some more shall we", as they both hugged each other. Declan entered the kitchen, "What is going on in here, everyone is dying of thirst out here" …

As they all sat around drinking their coffee, Sara announced that John was to rent the big Beach House up the coast for 3 months as they were contemplating a big move on the Coast. John mentioned that his company were expanding to Durham and as Sara loves it here so much and loves being near her sister, it was decided that he would rent the beach house for now, see how things go. Sara wanted to see how they settled first, but it seems like John is determined to make a go of it, he was of the view that they would buy a property along the coast road eventually… Jacqueline could not be happier. The evening was turning out to be a night to remember in all ways. Jacqueline felt that she had gained another sister in Serena, after they heartfelt conversation.

Declan stood up, "It's that time, it's time for some music and dancing, all requests will be playing in order", as he laughed walking to the record selection; Andy Williams, Johnny Mathis, Elvis Presley, The Beatles, The Four Tops, Diana Ross, Dusty Springfield, The Drifters, Chuck Berry. They danced every sort of dance, from the jive to the soul dancing and then the good fashioned waltz.

John pointed out that he had never enjoyed himself so much, and as they all departed Dylan asked Serena to walk along the beach with him, he was getting rather nervous as he had a very important box in his pocket that was burning a hole in his trousers all day!". Dylan had already got permission of Serena's father earlier on that day, and as soon as he had that permission he went swiftly to the jewellers. He knew Serena loved orchids, and she also loved daisies. He knew when he saw the daisy shaped diamonds that was the one.

They returned to the beachy head this time, towards Trow Rocks, a little spot of enclosed sandy beach which was a romantic spot and as Dylan turned to Serena, he bent on one knee and said, "I have a very important question to ask you, will you marry me and make me the happiest man alive?". Serena was overcome with such emotion, such overwhelming emotion! She hadn't a clue this was going to happen today…. Serena wept with joy and said, "Yes, yes! Yes! I will marry you! The ring was 18ct gold with a cluster of diamonds shaped like a daisy. Serena loved it so much. Dylan swept her off her feet and carried her into the sea and swung her around and around shouting "She will! She will! marry me! Onlookers stood clapping and clapping.

Chapter 16

As Serena returned home, all the lights were out, her parents had retired for the night, and she would have to wait until breakfast to tell them the great news of her forthcoming marriage. "I wonder how dad will take the news?", she murmured to herself, as she knew her mum would be elated as she had taken to Dylan like a duck to water. Serena yawned and got herself into bed, she slept like a baby.

The next morning Serena could not wait to see her parents, as she rushed down the stairs, her father shouted, "What's the hurry girl, you be careful of that third tread, it's still a bit tricky". Serena walked towards her father and kissed him, he looked confused? "What is that for he wondered?". Dad, I am going to be married, her father replied, "I know!". "How do you know?", Serena replied. Her father stood smirking away, "Dylan asked my permission a few days ago actually". Serena beamed with joy, "Oh dad, I am so glad you approve, it means the world to me ". They both had tears in their eyes, Serena's mum entered the room and said, "What is all this about you two, as if I didn't know, she smiled with tears in her eyes. So, my beautiful daughter, when is the big day to happen. "Oh mum, we haven't decided yet. I would like a spring wedding next year which is only 7 months away, that should give you two enough time to plan as I know you like to plan, Serena laughed out loud and turned to dad, "It's time dad to hit the office soon", Serena was always the conscientious one, her father loved her for that. He had big plans for Serena, as he was sure she was partnership material.

In the meantime, at the Gibson household Dylan let everyone know his big news. Jacqueline and Declan were more than happy. Colm was only interested in his big day at the shipyard with his Uncle Dylan, he rose early to be ready to be driven by Dylan. Colm was too excited to be nervous on his first Dylan. Dylan pointed out that it would be an easy day for him to be shown around the shipyard and the office, Colm was to shadow Dylan for a couple of weeks. He would be fetching and carrying for the lads initially until he was familiar with the workings of the ships coming into drydock. Colm was more than happy to muck in, he was enthusiastic about everything. Dylan turned to Colm, "Let's hope you stay this enthusiastic lad during your training, it's hard work but very rewarding ". Colm was keen to show Dylan how committed he was to his apprenticeship.

As they made their way onto the "Primrose" ship which had just come in for repair. Colm was taken below deck to the engine room where it all happens, he was fascinated by the shear length and size of the engines. He was introduced to the engineers working there, he hadn't realised that Dylan was one of the Senior Engineers, there were three of them and several young engineers of which Colm with be part of when he has completed his training.

They ventured into the Galley where the smell of food was making Colm hungry. We can have breakfast in five young un, "Don't worry we will get you fed before we crack on", as Dylan winked at Colm. The breakfast was mighty, a full English. Colm was stuffed and was ready to walk it off. They both went above and walked the length of the ship which was approximately 800 feet.

Dylan and Colm spent the morning on deck, upper and lower deck and ended the morning on the bridge where all the navigation takes place. It was a very productive morning for Colm as Dylan had to tick all the boxes for Colm's first induction day.

As they made their way up to the gang plank towards the office, which was a purpose-built building for all the draughtsman and office staff. Colm was hoping that he would not be in there long as he knew his dad would be seated in one of the offices. He felt a little embarrassed, Dylan assured him that he is now a working lad and shouldn't let it bother him, as he would have to work in there as part of his apprenticeship. Colm was more interested in the art of how the ship was built and the engine rooms. As they walked into to the office, they were met by the Senior Manager Matt who explained to Colm that he would have to file papers and fetch and carry from everyone during his two-week training in the office. Colm was hoping that the two weeks would fly over quickly…

Dylan turned to Colm, let's start you in the office tomorrow and we can get that over with as I know you want to get to the ship. Colm sighed but was happy to go along with things as they stood. Declan his dad pointed out that it was not all boring in the office, wait until you experience how we do our drawings, that might appeal to you more Colm. As Colm listened to his dad, he became a little more interested, especially about how the drawings were made up, after all, he thought, it is art, and he liked to draw, it may not be that bad he murmured to himself… Colm's Induction day came to an end and he felt that his career was meant to be aboard a ship, he was sure of that. He couldn't wait to get home and tell his mam all about it. Jacqueline was so proud of her son, and she felt such joy that he was staying at home, at least I have two at home, as her thoughts turned to Niamh and the fact that her daughter Niamh was only a few days way from travelling to Dunston University to live in the halls. Jacqueline was not convinced it was a good idea, but she knew in heart that Niamh was determined to study alongside her friends, Katie, and Jessica, as they both were arriving on the same day as Niamh.

Niamh was already busy packing away her books and clothes in readiness for the big day… Emily was happy for Niamh as she had worked hard to get to Dunston University, and she knew how much it meant to her. Emily was now established in her new role at the Wool Shop and wanted Niamh to have that same contentment she had. Emily was always of the view that Niamh would go far and even travel as she was more adventurous than herself. Emily would always be a home bird.

Everything was going too fast in Jacqueline's mind, she just couldn't get her head around her family growing so fast, "When did this all happen?", she thought to herself, it just seems like yesterday when we moved into this beach cottage, which was in fact well over 10 years. Jacqueline had her moment to herself once again, where she sauntered down to the beach and sat at her favourite spot at Trow Rocks. How blessed I am as she looked up into the blue sky, the memories of her mother and father came flooding back to her like a dream, as she recalled her childhood and the moment when they were all at the beach and her father was playing football, What a tomboy I was, always with my father. Mother sitting with our Aileen and Sara joining in with the football game. Oh! Jacqueline sighed, such happiness. Jacqueline couldn't stand her deep feelings of loss at the moment, it was as if her Mother and Father were still here... Oh how we reminisce so, I must pull myself together and think of it as change a good change, a happy change as Niamh is so happy and there is nothing more exhilarating as seeing her children so happy, Jacqueline smiled at herself and began thinking of a poem she wanted to created ;

The Heart of the Matter, Jacqueline began to write, she always had a pen and paper with her when she ventured to her favourite spot at the beach, she sat in the alcove near Trow Rocks and scribbled away ...

The journey end that comes to light...
Our hearts are heavy but their future is bright..

Our hearts keep beating like a drum..
A change of style will be a happy overcome...
For destiny is a speckle of light that burns so bright..

Special moments that will live on...
For the Heart of the Matter is so strong...

I like that Jacqueline read it back to herself, yes, I will put that in my journey folder with the rest of the poems. Jacqueline jumped up, Ooh! It's time to get back to reality and back to the kitchen, a hearty meal tonight as Niamh will be away tomorrow. Let's celebrate a great future, as Jacqueline smiled and sauntered back to the cottage, the day was warm and the seagulls were in flight; a beautiful pasta dish tonight, as it was Niamh's favourite.

Sara was at the back door with news of her forthcoming long stay at the beach house down the road. It turned out to be a special day as her sister and husband announced they were moving here for good. Jacqueline began to cry, and Sara put her arms around her sister, "What is this Sis", as she looked into her eyes." It's Niamh isn't it your beautiful daughter leaving home the first one to leave home, I know you Sis like the back of my hand. "Yes, I had a moment earlier, but my poetry saved me ", Jacqueline went onto the read the poem, and Sara loved it and said, "Never stop writing Jacqueline, I think that is your therapy of life. I think you are right Sara, Jacqueline replied. As they went into the cottage, Sara explained to Jacqueline that John was setting up a business in Newcastle and Sara was going to check out the local hospitals as she had previously been a nurse and was looking for a part time position to keep her busy at it. They had no children as Sara and John were not maternal and loved their holidays abroad.

As the day progressed, Colm was getting into his stride and the Shipyard and Declan was keeping a low profile so his son could find his own way around and it seemed to be working. Emily was holding a wool sale so the customers could get their favourite patterns, it was a very busy week for Emily. The Gibson's family all seem to be settling with fact that Niamh was leaving them, although Colm was looking forward to the party, he loved his food, Jacqueline had to include a good piece of fish on the menu as Colm loved his fish and chips. Pasta was not one of his favourites...

Everything was ready and everyone gathered in the garden as Declan and Colm got the big tables and chairs out. Sara, John, Dylan, and Serena had arrived it was a big family occasion. Jacqueline kept herself busy in the kitchen. Niamh spent some time with her mother and assured her that she would come home some weekends to see her, "Even if it is just to bring my washing home", Niamh chuckled to her mother. Jacqueline put her arm around her daughter and said, "I don't mind when you come home, as long as you are happy pet, that is what makes me very happy ". They both embraced and got a little emotional as Sara entered the kitchen she said, "Ooh I will have to join in with all this cuddling and kissing". They all embraced and Declan once again, got the music going, Niamh wanted the Beatles on, and her dad didn't disappoint. They danced the night away. Colm invited his friend Tom and they ventured on to the beach to chat about their work experiences, Tom went into the local garage to train as a mechanic, they had lots to talk about.

Dylan and Serena announced the wedding would take place on the 11th of April 1970. It was settled, the venue, they were going to have to think about that, Serena's mother will probably have already had somewhere in mind, so Serena would have to keep an eye on that one....

Chapter 17

The day had arrived, and Niamh was up bright and early, as Jacqueline and Declan greeted her at the bottom of the stairs. "Wow Mam and Dad, you already dressed". "Look at you, you are all grown up all of a sudden", as Jacqueline hugged her daughter. They all had breakfast, and Emily said her goodbyes to her sister knowing that she would come home with her washing as Niamh was so tidy and presentable, washing was a must where Niamh was concerned. Colm gave his sister a hug and went off to his third day of induction at the shipyard.

Declan had the car ready, and they were off, as they drove into the drive of the university, Jacqueline thought it looked bigger than when they visited early that year. It had beautiful landscape gardens and a lake at the back. The courtyard was very majestic. The library stood high up on the hill like an eagle in flight, those revolving doors reminded Jacqueline of something out the movies...

There were plenty of facilities, such as the book shop of course and there was the student's union where all the students hung out. The chapel was very Victorian, it looked as though it had stepped back in time, but looked so magnificent it is leafy outbuilding.

Jacqueline stood back and took a picture of the Chapel with her old-fashioned camera, Declan chuckled, "You and that old camera". Jacqueline smiled, "My dad's camera will live forever". They all made their way to the infamous library, Niamh was telling her mam and dad that the range of books far outweighed the nearby libraries they would visit, and other local universities use the facilities at Dunston. Declan was impressed as they went into the library. There were three floors, the literature section was on the third floor. Niamh was showing her mam and dad the selection of books she was going to read for her degree, namely, The Romantic Poets, Keats, Shelly, Bryan, Coleridge, and

Wordsworth. Niamh was interested in the period of 18c and 19c novelist such as Jane Austen, the Bronte sisters and Elizabeth Gaskell. Jacqueline was having a peak at Alexander Pope works, the great poet of the 18c, she was fascinated with rhyming couplet of his poem; Ode on solitude, his happy view of solitude is nature bound in every sense of the word, both physical and domestic. Jacqueline loved this poem.

Niamh was watching her mam and thought, "Why didn't mam take her enthusiasm of literature further?". Jacqueline looked across at Niamh and said, "I think you will flourish here pet, I really do". Niamh put her arm around her mam and said, "I think you would have too mam years ago". Jacqueline pointed out to Niamh that she was so happy having met Declan and had children and wouldn't have it any other way. Declan was having a wander around the library and was in the history and maths section he was enjoying flicking through the masterpieces of Great Britain and the two World Wars and the of course the great ships. Declan could have stayed in the library all day, as he was happy to sit and read; he had never seen such a large selection of history books.

As they all caught up with one and another, Declan suggested a spot of lunch before they took Niamh to her dormitory. They headed to the main restaurant, which was situated in the Howston Building, it was a very big restaurant sectioned into three elements, one for snacks and a coffee shop and the other two sections were main meals and selection of help yourself to pasta or salads. They opted to have a main meal, the tables were very well set out with white tablecloths and have and little flower arrangement which looked rather quaint, Jacqueline thought to herself. There were lots on the menu, Declan went for the meat pie, Jacqueline went for the fish, and Niamh went for the pasta dish. It was all delicious. "I think it's time we took you to your dormitory and let you get on my pet", as Declan put his arm around Niamh. Jacqueline stomach dropped a little, she was feeling that emotional feeling again, Jacqueline was determined to keep herself in check and not get too emotional.

As they made their way to the dormitory Niamh's friends' Jessica and Kate had arrived with their parents. They all sat in the foyer area of the Howston building chatting away about the university and its campus. All agreed that it was a great place for their children to study. It was time to make their way to the individual rooms, Niamh, Jessica, and Kate made sure when they applied that their rooms would be next to each other.

Jacqueline opened the door to Niamh's room and was surprised to see it was quite spacious, as walked into the room there was a large bookcase to the left with a decent bed and mattress next to it, a small sideboard, like a dresser. In the window was oak desk with plenty of drawers. An armchair to relax in. Niamh was well pleased with her room and the campus. As she hugged her mam and dad and said her goodbyes, "I will see you next weekend, ok". Declan took Jacqueline by the hand and led her out of the room. As they both walked down the corridor Declan squeezed Jacqueline's hand and said, "Niamh will be fine here love; you will get used with it, give a few months and you will settle into it". Jacqueline was feeling a little more relaxed as she had seen her daughter settled and her friends nearby.

The drive home was melancholy, they both felt that strange feeling of separation. Declan and Jacqueline both agreed they would not dwell on it. Declan dropped Jacqueline off at the Church Centre so she could catch up with the reading group for their next session on Thursday. Declan headed back to work.

Patricia and Gloria were falling out as to what they should read for Thursday, Jacqueline gave out a smile at the corner of her mouth and muttered to herself, "Ooh how good it is to be back in the realm again, or not. They all sat down around the big table, Jacqueline listened to everyone's recommendations for the next book to read, and it was unanimous that they would like to read Elizabeth Gaskells novel, 'Ruth' about a young, orphaned seamstress. They all decided to meet up next month to discuss the novel. Jacqueline was feeling animated as she loved this novel and wouldn't mind reading it again.

Sara, Jacqueline's sister appeared at the centre to call on Jacqueline as she had some great news to share. Sara had secured a post at the local hospital 3 days a week. Jacqueline left Patricia and Gloria to it, for Gloria would always get the upper hand where Patricia was concerned, although Gloria had been very mellow these days because of Patricia's loss of her husband. It had been 6 months now since the mining accident and everyone was getting on with it. Patricia was getting back to her argumentative self once again and didn't Gloria know about it... They were in fact inseparable, and fed off each other's arguments, it was the highlight of their day.

Sara suggested that they head to the Beach to Sanders for a celebratory drink, after all it was a celebration as Sara had secured a position at the local hospital even though there were quite a lot of candidates, she was so determined to make her mark in South Shields. They had a leisurely afternoon reminiscing about when they were young, Jacqueline the tomboy always hanging out with her dad. Sara the adventurous one always going missing down to the parks, anywhere that had a lot of activity, Sara was more outgoing than Jacqueline. "Who would have thought us two ending up living next to each other", as Sara pointed out to her sister Jacqueline. Although Jacqueline always thought that Sara would move away as she was the more adventurous and presumed, she would live down South as it was much warmer, as she loved the sun and sunbathing. Jacqueline hoped that Sara would settle for good in South Shields, as there wasn't a finer beach or coastline to be had, just as good as down South, that was Jacqueline view; the north is as good as the South where beaches were concerned.

As they drank a toast to the future, "Here is to happiness and success for us all", Sara raised her glass and Jacqueline joined in. For what is family, but togetherness as they were a close family there was no doubt about that.

They got so carried away and were engrossed in conversation, and lost track of time, they hadn't realised that they had been sitting in the bistro for over 2 hours. "My word Sara its almost 4pm, I better make tracks Declan and Colm will be home soon", as Jacqueline stood up. "It's been a wonderful day Jacqueline", Sara looked lovingly at her sister. "Yes, my beautiful sis, it has", Jacqueline replied. For Sara was a beauty, she was the belle of ball since she was a youngster, with her off blonde hair and her slight figure, Jacqueline was always a bit jealous of how much Sara could eat but never put weight on, mind you, Sara doesn't sit still enough to put weight on.

Jacqueline returned home to get the evening meal ready for the family, she started to sing a little as prepared the meal, as it was such an extraordinary day, from saying Goodbye to Niamh and meeting up with Sara and getting the book club on track. Jacqueline was feeling exhilarated by it all and decided to make a large quiche and a corned beef pie with plucky potato salad to accompany it all.

In the meantime, back at the wool shop Emily's sale was going down a storm she was so busy, and Aileen had suggested that Emily take on a work experience young lady to support her in the shop. Emily would make enquiries at the local schools to see if any of the young ladies would be interested in embarking on a career at a Sales Assistant. The feedback Emily was receiving was such a surprise she had no idea that some many were interested in sales and the creative ideas that come with working in a wool shop. Emily thought to herself, "I am offering a creative career in a way, because not only do we produce good things out of wool, but we also create garments and toys from many ways, such as the knitting aspect of the wool and the cross stitch, and tapestry we also sell. As Emily murmured to herself, "We are offering a young adult a great career". Emily started to hum her favourite tune, 'What a wonderful world".

The day was closing, and Emily couldn't be happier with the outcome. Emily's dear friend Louisa bought so much wool, as she also loved to cross stitch. They both decided to have a night out together as they hadn't been out for ages and planned to go out on Friday night which was only a few days away.

The Gibson household was full of laughter and good news for all. Colm was in great spirits he was loving every minute at the shipyard. Declan glanced at Jacqueline as their eyes met it was if they were as one as they both were thinking the same thing; it was going to be one of their romantic nights together once everyone had gone to bed.

It was much later, as Declan and Jacqueline went for a romantic stroll along the beach, hand in hand discussing the day's events and how so in love they were 18 years of marriage, it seems like yesterday Declan thought to himself. They took a slow walk back to the cottage and went upstairs to bed, it was a loving night to remember.... as they clung to each other.

Chapter 18

Colm was getting ready for his big day in the office with his father, everyone was so amazed that Colm was the first one up on this bright and sunny morning. Dylan was busy supervising the new ship that had just come in, "Arctic Zone" and there was no time for him to spend with Colm today. Colm would have to put up with his dad on this day. Colm was getting quite interested in the aspect of being a draughtsman like his dad. That was Declan's plan as he felt it would be a safer career than working on a ship, as there had been a few accidents in the past years on various ships.

As Colm sat alongside his dad, he began to understand the ratios and dimensions of how to create a drawing; the frame and spacing of a ship. Colm would have to learn the line plan, body plan, the waterlines, and the profile of a ship. The plan is to get Colm to be able to read a ship plan confidently with its complex curves. it was going to take some time, maybe 6 months at least before he can have a go on his own, but he was quite prepared to wait his turn. Declan was recovering well from his mining accident and his check-ups all went well, he was so content in his new role at the shipyard, and now his son alongside him has made him even more content.

Jacqueline's day was also going well, as she was helping her sis to look for a permanent home nearby as the beach house was lovely, but it was a small complex with very little room, more like a holiday chalet type property. They both decided to venture down to the Estate Agents as Sara had already viewed a lovely property, Byrant's Cottage not too far from Jacqueline's it was 500 yards up the Coast Road, set back, in Byrant View, a quaint little side road with only four cottages along it.

As they approached the Estate Agents in town, they both looked at each other and said, "Here goes, let's hope they will accept £3,500.00, as Sara and John had discussed that £3,500 was their best offer. Mr Rothwell the Estate Agent greeted them with a big smile, "Would you both like a cup of tea of coffee". They both spoke at the same time, "Yes, coffee please". He smiled and his assistant Joanne obliged. Mr Rothwell brought out the Sale Agreement and the Vendor's instructions on how much they would accept. Sara and Jacqueline looked on with amazement to find that £3,5000.00 would be acceptable in this instance, Sara was beaming. Mr Rothwell replied, "Are we satisfied with the contents, if so, let's go ahead with the deal. Mr Rothwell asked which legal firm Sara was using. Sara replied, "Oh I have not looked into that yet?". "No problem, we can appoint one for you", Mr Rothwell replied. Jacqueline stepped in and said, "We can sort that out, we do have a close friend who is a Solicitor, we will get back to you later today".

As Sara and Jacqueline left the office, Jacqueline said, "We will call Serena and see if she can help us out on this". Sara was delighted. They arrived back at the cottage and telephoned Serena; Serena did have conveyancing experience as she was a corporate lawyer, and it was not a problem for Serena to represent them. Serena told Sara to get the Estate Agents to contact her directly. Serena was adamant that they would only have to pay for the Land Registry fees, Coal mining search and bankruptcy searches, her fees were free. Sara was overcome by this and took the telephone off Jacqueline and said, "Serena, I must pay something, I insist". Serena pointed out that she could buy a wedding present next year that would suffice. Sara was happy to oblige and asked Serena to send her the wedding list.

The transaction would take about 6 to 8 weeks to complete as the searches would be at least 6 weeks; Serena notified them both that the Coal Mining Search usually takes longer to come back. Sara was very happy with the outcome. Sara and Jacqueline decided to venture to Newcastle and have a shopping spree and enjoy themselves. They both bought luxurious items at Faram's and Ben's. Jacqueline was feeling guilty as Sara insisted that she would treat Jacqueline to a lovely dress from Farams. "I will pay for lunch at Lacey's then, no arguments Sara", as Jacqueline squeezed her sister's hand. Lacey's was a classy little bistro on the corner of Nevine Street, how devilishly extravagant they had been today. Let's keep that to ourselves shall we as Sara turned to Jacqueline, they walked down Nevine Street giggling like two teenagers. "I think we better head Home Sara", as Jacqueline tugged her arm, "You have spent enough today, and we have had the best time". "Ok spoil sport", as Sara reluctantly agreed.

They both decided to stop off at the Wool Shop to see how Emily was coping with the Sale this week. Sara was interested in buying some tapestry for the beach house, she loved a good piece of tapestry. Emily had taken on Belinda as her new assistant, she was very presentable, a little shy, but Emily was going to bring the best of her; the sale would do that as the shop was busy every hour.

Emily told Belinda to see to Sara in her purchase for a tapestry piece, Emily pointed out to Belinda that should ask the customer which pattern of tapestry she was interested, a portrait or a flower design, or a landscape design, trees, or fields maybe. Sara was impressed by Belinda's friendly mannerism, even though she looked a little nervous. "I love that horse and cart design in the field, and I will also take the lovely flowerpot design you have there". Belinda had made her first two sales, and she was smiling with delight. Emily knew she had picked the right candidate to assist in the shop. Belinda was going to be a great asset as she was so keen and willing. Emily pointed out that she didn't need to come to work so early, Belinda was happy to come early.

Sara couldn't wait for John to get home and give him the good news. John was so pleased as he liked the cottage so much too. "Let's celebrate", as John turned to Sara. "Oh, John there is a celebration going on tonight, sorry Jacqueline and I set it up earlier, I hope you don't mind love". "Mind, oh no the more the merrier", as John smiled back at Sara. Serena and Dylan are also invited but our Niamh will be missing as Jacqueline sighed, even though she had received a telephone call from Niamh to say that she had settled into her studies and was loving it. Niamh had told her mam that she would not be home for the weekend as they were having a "fresher's weekend at the Student Union". There were washing facilities on campus for them to wash their clothes. Jacqueline was a little disappointed, but she knew she would have to get used with the idea.

Jacqueline decided to concentrate on the night ahead and plan the buffet for all, Sara was only too happy to supply some food too, a joint effort for all. Emily entered in the room and quietly had a word with her mam. "Mam I am not going to be in tonight, as I have made arrangements to go out with Louisa tonight, I cannot let her down now". Jacqueline smiled and said, "Of course not pet, you go and enjoy yourself". Colm also, pointed out he was going round to Tom's house. Jacqueline prepared for adult night. It was in fact going to be a family night, as Jacqueline's two sisters Aileen and Sara were coming. Jacqueline smiled to herself, and reminded herself that the three of them hadn't been together for a meal for a while. "I best make the most of it", as she muttered to herself.

Sara came into the room with lots of food, Pasta, fish dishes. Jacqueline supplied the meat pies and quiches and corned beef pie, and of course a two large trifles. Sara would make up a punch bowl as it was an auspicious occasion for both Sara and John. Declan responded by saying, "What a great idea Sara, mind you us lads will stick to the whiskey later", as she smiled and winked at Jacqueline as he brushed her shoulder.

As everyone had arrived, including Dylan and Serena, Sara and her sisters were eager to have a look at Serena's wonderful engagement ring. Sara couldn't help but make a comment on it, "Wow Serena it so elegant and suits your finger". Serena was so pleased to be able to have a proper conversation with Jacqueline's sisters. As they all sat around the table eating and drinking that lovely punch Sara made, they all became animated with the alcohol so there was no stopping Sara engaging into the conversation about her fabulous purchase. John was so pleased too. Serena was explaining that she and Dylan had not made up their minds about a venue for their future wedding, however, her mother was getting rather ambitious. Jacqueline and Sara suggested that the Lake House was a prominent venue, as it was just off the coast road and, of course there is a beautiful lake, hence, the Lake House. Serena was so intrigued and was going to give them a ring for a visit and to have a look what they had to offer. Aileen responded by letting Serena know that she and her husband Arthur had attend a function there last year and it was rather spectacular, also, the food was amazing. Serena's eyes lit up, "Oh that's for us Dylan, that sounds like our venue". Dylan replied, "Mmm what about your mam?". "Oh, don't worry sweetie, I will sort my mum out". "What about your dad Serena.". "My dad, I can persuade to do anything", Dylan gave a wry smile, "I forgot how you can twist your dad round your little finger, ha ha ". Jacqueline and Declan laughed out loud and said, "Sounds like you have got this all sorted, no drama".

Jacqueline began to wonder how Emily was getting on in town, as she wasn't one for going out that much. Emily and Louisa had arrived at the Lantern bistro by the beach, which was buzzing, they managed to grab a couple of stools near the small stage where there were going to be a performance by the Triton duo; a saxophone player and a piano player, a bit of blues and jazz by the looks of it as Louisa scanned the board for drinks and lite bite to eat.

As they both sat on their stools two lads walked by one named Frankie, who gave a cheeky wink at Emily, "Did you see that Louisa, he thinks he is someone special". Louisa replied, "sounds like you may have scored Emily". "Really it takes more than a wink to impress me Louisa". "What does impress you, Emily?". "I like a young man with good personality, but with good manners too, I don't want someone who thinks they can take advantage from the start". "You are well rounded then, no flies on you as Louisa laughed.", "I know, Emily laughed", Emily was no fool, her Mam brought her up to look out for herself.

Frankie stood at the bar ordering a drink, he was of medium height, well dressed in his polo shirt and slacks, dark hair, and hazel eyes, Emily had noticed that. He turned and smiled at Emily; Emily looked away she didn't want to look as though she was interested, she was feeling rather shy and embarrassed now, as Emily hadn't really had much experience where boys were concerned, but she did learn a lot from her sister Niamh who was very popular with the boys, Niamh always shrugged them off and laughed at them. Emily was going to repeat that approach as she felt safe that way.

Frankie and his mate Ian decided to grab two stools quite hear Emily and Louisa. Frankie was bold one, "Hello girls, how is your night going, looking forward to the Tritons coming on". Emily pretended she didn't hear him, Louisa replied, "We are good thanks". Ian turned to Frankie, "They are not interested mate, give over mate". Frankie supped his pint and was not going to be dismayed by the brush off. He would bide his time and hope that he would be able to speak to Emily before the night was over.

The Tritons came on and everyone was dancing and singing, Frankie was determined to get next to Emily, as he approached her, he said, "I am trying too hard, am I putting you off". Emily was taken back by his boldness, his cheeky grin, she laughed, "Don't try too hard, it does put me off". Frankie felt the tone in Emily's voice and the wry smile gave him hope. Frankie could see he was chatting to a classy lass, and he wasn't going to blow it not for a minute.

At the end of the night, he asked Emily for her phone number, but she was reluctant to give that out at this stage. "Perhaps we will see each other again here". "Next Friday!", Frankie looked hopeful. "Maybe", Emily replied.

Chapter 19

Jacqueline was looking at the clock, it's getting late Declan, "Come on pet she is 19 years old; you know Emily is sensible, let her enjoy herself, its only 11.30pm". As Declan finished speaking to Jacqueline the door opened and in came Emily. Jacqueline sighed with relief and asked if she had a good night, "It was great mam, the Tritons were on, and they were fabulous". "Aww glad you had a good time pet". Declan looked at Jacqueline with that look of, "I told you so" …

As Emily went into her bedroom, she was rather intrigued by this Frankie but wasn't going to let it take over her thoughts. Louisa wanted to go back to the bistro next Friday as she rather liked his pal Ian, so it was settled they were going back the next Friday.

As Declan and Jacqueline settled into bed, Jacqueline began to think of her other daughter Niamh, and how the "Freshers Weekend" was going. It was a weekend where all the new students would get together, lots of entertainment was put on in various parts of the campus, to accommodate everyone's tastes in different classes of music, Rock, Soul, Classical, Pop.

Declan reminded Jacqueline that she had done a marvellous job bringing up their 3 children who are all capable of looking after themselves. Jacqueline was such a worrier; she worried a lot. Declan had always been the calm one, the rock of the family as always managed to calm Jacqueline down; he recalled that time when Niamh had split her chin open when she was 6 years old when she fell off her bike. Jacqueline was in such a state and Declan had to be called out of the pit head as Jacqueline was not at all good with injuries especially when it came to her daughter or son for that matter. Declan was swift to take Niamh to hospital and she still has 5 stitches under her chin to this day.

Niamh was having a ball with her newfound freedom at the Student Union, with her two pals, Kate, and Jessica. The Student Union was a large building Ground Floor was the bar and the first floor was the stage for venues, bands playing, and the third floor was the Drama Society where all the plays took place.

Kate was making friends fast as she was extrovert of them all. They all met quite a few students in their year, both male and female, some were quite posh, and others had similar backgrounds to them. Niamh was of the view that everyone was equal no matter what background you came from, for what does it matter; the only thing that matters is how you were brought up, if you didn't have good manners and good values, then Niamh was not interested at all, for Jacqueline and Declan had brought Niamh up to respect her elders and always be polite and caring towards others even if you don't agree with them. Niamh was rather naïve at university as she had no idea how this was going to turn out.

The Fresher's weekend at the Student Union got off with a bang, there were around 3.000 students on the upper floor where the entertainment was about to start. First on was a compare who introduced the first band who were the 'Astronauts', a rock band. The ballroom as it used to be known was rocking, the sound was deafening. Niamh and her friends were not really into rock bands, they all preferred soul and jazz. They decided to opt for the bar downstairs until the soul band 'The moonlighters', came on. Niamh, Jessica, and Kate, weighed into the crowd and eventually got to the bar. It was Niamh's first experience with alcohol as she sampled her first baby cham drink; she wasn't sure whether she liked it or not but would go with the flow, as Jessica and Kate were lapping them up. There was a certain electrifying buzz around campus. Jessica was off, her first encounter with a male student Josh who was from Buckinghamshire, he looked very studious with his book under his arm; a squatter no doubt. Jessica was intrigued by his accent, but not so much with his conversation, as all he talked about was science and mathematics. Jessica got rid of him rather quickly. Niamh and Kate giggled away at Jessica's antics, they couldn't believe Jessica, as she was up for anything. "Why did you lead him on, it was obvious you weren't interested?" Kate piped up. "I liked his accent and was hoping he would match it, but what a big let-down", Kate gave Jessica a look. "What are you like, the poor lad". "Ooh he will get over it, properly looking for the next one to chat up as we speak, boys are so fickle , Jessica was convinced of that.

As the three of them browsed around the room to find that empty corner they could lay their drinks down. They ended up taking the drinks on the deck which was built on at the rear of the building it was a large deck with plenty of seating. They had lit it up with small bauble lighting, which was quite romantic, as Niamh observed with great interest. Niamh was the dreamer, the poet who saw poetry in almost everything. Kate was the realistic one who was only interested in facts, for she loved history and was drawn to the facts of historical aristocracy. The three of them would be reading Shakespeare in their first year, Kate with the facts, Niamh with her interest in the romantic poets' although the romantic poets were not as we know it, for romantic poets were not seen in the academic world as romance but rather as a movement for the Arts which originated from the 18th century. Niamh was looking forward to studying the Romantic Poets, especially, John Keats, Lord Byron, Percy Shelley, and Samuel Taylor Coleridge. Jessica was more interested in period designs, and that was the only reason she was tempted to go for this module with her best friends. Jessica was always intrigued by everything.

As they all sat together, they were spotted by three young men coming towards them, James, Andrew, and Ben. They looked like they were already in the party mood. James the blond lad from Wiltshire, Andrew was from Edinburgh he was the dark tall handsome one, and cheeky Ben from the Pembrokeshire, they were all very well spoken.

Ben and Jessica were the first to hit it off as they both couldn't stop talking. James approached Kate and asked if she would like to dance as everyone on deck was apparently dancing to the DJ's music, they had set up outside. Andrew was quite happy sitting next to Niamh as they talked about their ambitions and what they would like to do when they finished their degree. Andrew was hoping to go into Architecture as he loved buildings, and his father was a well-known architect. Andrew was fascinated to hear about Niamh's passion for literature and poetry, he found her quite alluring.

The hours went by, and it was time to say our good nights, the lads were all very gentleman like and walked the ladies to their dormitories. Once Jessica, Kate, and Niamh were behind doors they all sat in Niamh's room and talked until the early hours. Jessica found Ben so funny, and she liked his personality, he was studying English language. Kate was not that bothered about James, as he was so into himself and his image, not Kate's idea of a good date at all, she declined a further invitation to meet up again. Niamh, however, was quite taken with Andrew, who wouldn't be, he was well built, dark haired and handsome, and seem to have caring characteristics, however, Niamh was adamant that she would not get romantically attached to anyone, as she did not want to be distracted from her degree. Niamh was hoping to teach once she had a good degree under her belt. For Niamh did not want any complications in her life whilst she was at university. Jessica was quite the opposite as she was clever in her own right, but Jessica had to have fun at any cost. Kate was looking for her ideal mate, and she was hoping to meet him at university, but Kate would have to wait that bit longer. I have 3 years here, plenty of time. The girls vowed and made a pact that they would stay as best friends and keep in touch after their university days.

It was almost 10am before they awoke, after all, they did not go to sleep until 3am in the morning. It was a new dawn for all of them as they were away from home and didn't have to get up at 8 in the morning, at least, not until Monday when classes start. A leisurely day it is, it's a Sunday and Niamh was happy that Dunston Chapel service was at 11am on campus, very thoughtful of them Niamh smiled to herself. Kate and Jessica stayed in bed and Niamh ventured down the pathway passed the beautiful landscapes surrounding the campus. The leafy Chapel stood out

113

as the sunshine slithered across the crevices of the front side of the Chapel. It brought nature alive as the leaves glistened and swaggered across the front entrance of the Chapel. It was quite large in the main hall of the Chapel, but there was a small section that was detached which had a sign on it, 'Study groups'.

Niamh thought of her mam at that moment and knew her mam would love this Chapel, "I must get mam to come one weekend to see for herself". Niamh was seated and Fr Kershaw was very vibrant with his service and very academic with it. All the students were given a booklet about the Chapel and it events, as there were classical concerts once a month that took place. Niamh happened on a poster that read, "Poetry Evenings Thursday at 7pm", as she gazed with delight at that prospect. Niamh decided to call her mam once she was back in dormitory. There were two telephones in the hallways, so hopefully she would be able to get to one of them.

Meanwhile back at the Gibson's Jacqueline could not stop thinking how Niamh was getting on with hr first weekend at university. "I suppose I will have to let this go sooner rather than later", she whispered to herself as she was hanging the washing out. Declan was reading his paper as he always did on a Sunday looking up the latest crossword puzzle. He too, in his own right was hoping Niamh was having a good time.

Just as Jacqueline was entering the back door the telephone rang, "It's Niamh Declan", Jacqueline cried out. "How are you doing pet, everything ok?", "Yes, Mam, couldn't be better, I thought I would give you a quick call as there is a bit of queue here, so I will be quick, the Chapel is amazing mam, and you must come over one Sunday to meet Fr Kershaw he is so funny and very intelligent, I must go , ring you next week". Jacqueline was calmed now; she was settled in her mind and in her stomach, and Declan was relieved about that. "Our daughter is settled Declan, and I couldn't be happier" as she snuggled up to her husband.

114

Emily walked in the room in laughing, "You two snuggling on a Sunday, really mam and dad" Declan winked at Emily as he got up to make a cup of tea. Colm was already out and down the Beach, drawing his famous seagull that keeps coming back to the same rock at Trow Rocks. Colm decided to call him Flick, as he flickered up and down on that rock and it was hard for Colm to keep a grasp of his drawing, so he drew this seagull every Sunday, he had a book full of Flick, as he shouted to Flick, "Keep still Flick! How am I supposed to get your best side lad". Flick seem to acknowledge Colm, as he looked very majestic and tilted his head up and down, mmm, Colm turned to him, "Flick sit still a minute". Colm was getting quite attached to him and it seemed that Flick was also always happy to see Colm it was as if he was sitting waiting for him on that infamous rock.

The sunshine was blistering away over Trow Rocks; the sea looked so serene in the sunlight. The sky was so blue not a cloud in sight. What a way to enjoy a Sunday, as Colm finished off his drawing. He sat awhile with Flick and wasn't sure if he was understanding him as chatted away to him, but there were moments when Flick would just stare at Colm and make a sound almost like a squeaking whistle and bow his head. "If only I could understand your sounds Flick, wouldn't that me something hey lad". Flick squeaked even more. Colm sat back and took in the view which was breathtaking, "Hey Flick it's great to just sit back and watch he waves – what I am doing talking to a seagull who has no idea what I am talking about, ooh I am hungry, it must be lunchtime…

Sunday lunch was ready at the Gibson's, their first Sunday lunch without Niamh, Colm was ready for his lunch the sea air had made him hungry. "Mam I will have Niamh's portion too he laughed ". Declan shouted up, "No you will not lad, we shall share Niamh's portion between us all, as I am the oldest, I get the biggest portion", as Declan winked at Colm. It had been a memorable weekend for all.

115

Chapter 20

Monday morning had arrived, it was busy morning, Emily was first to leave as she was still showing Belinda the ropes and wanted to get a head start. Declan and Colm followed out the door for their busy day at the office. Jacqueline was interrupted by a telephone call from Serena, who was hoping that Jacqueline would accompany her to the Lake House at 6pm that day, as she valued Jacqueline's opinion. Dylan was tied up with work, as the new ship, "Artic Zone", was not in good shape and needed a lot of work before it was fit to sail. Serena and Dylan decided that Jacqueline would be a great stand in for him. Although Jacqueline was confused, as she wondered why Serena had not asked her Mam to come along. It turned out that Charlotte had already made plans for a venue which was out at Durham, Bixham Hall. Serena explained to Jacqueline that her Mam was getting carried with the wedding plans, they chatted for some length and Serena would pick Jacqueline up at 5.30pm. As Jacqueline put the receiver down, she sat in the armchair thinking about Charlotte. "Oh, I hope Charlotte and Serena don't fall out over this?". Jacqueline had a plan; Jacqueline was always good at solving a tricky problem.

As Jacqueline mulled over the situation Serena had got herself into regarding the venue, "I will call Charlotte and ask her if she would like to attend the Art and Craft Exhibition at the Church Centre. "That's it, what a great plan", a mischievous smile came upon her face. The Exhibition was open that very afternoon, as she knew Charlotte love Arts and Crafts. As Jacqueline dialled the number, "I am doing the right thing", she said to herself, it's for a good cause. Charlotte picked up and she was delighted to attend the exhibition. It was settled they would meet at 2pm. "Ooh I need to come up with something extraordinary to convince Charlotte to come along to the Lake House later, I must get my thinking cap on quickly!".

Bixham Hall was out of the way, so there is a good point to raise as everyone would struggle to get to the venue, as the Lake House as good transport routes and its central for everyone to get to. The Lake House is more idyllic than the Hall, but the Hall is more majestic. Jacqueline wrote down the advantages and disadvantages of both venues; The Lake House advantages, romantic setting, its quaint rural beams, it's not far from the Beach. Dylan and Serena love the Beach. The catwalk of decking is mounted towards the lake, there is a great walkway which captures the beautiful trees. Whereas Bixham Hall is large, and the rooms have very tall ceilings, it has an emptiness about it. "Ooh let's just see how the afternoon goes first, as Jacqueline sauntered slowly to the Church Centre, a good walk along the pathway alongside the Beach will give me food for thought, as it always did where Jacqueline was concerned, her walks on the Beach always seem to come up with good solutions.

Charlotte arrived at the Centre, and was excited to view the lovely displays, and was keen to purchase some of them. There were great displays of Art, as some of the local artists do excellent paintings of the Lighthouse and Beach; there were some breathtaking pictures of Trow Rocks, and the coves that surround them. Charlotte purchased 2 paintings, one of the beaches and one of Trow Rocks, and stayed for coffee and cake. This was the moment for Jacqueline to approach the subject of weddings and events. Jacqueline put her pitch forward about the Lake House, and pointed out all the advantages of the Lake House, and Charlotte was intrigued. Charlotte went on to say that she had looked at Bixham Hall and was convinced that Serena would love that, and she was going to ask Serena to view it on Friday that week.

The conversation wasn't going the way Jacqueline had imagined... Jacqueline turned to Charlotte and smiled, "Dylan and Serena were most interested in my sister's views on the Lake House, and my oldest sister Aileen is a regular customer at the Lake House. Charlotte looked at Jacqueline and said "Oh, really, that's interesting, Serena never mentioned it?". "I am sure she will, it always a topsy turvy time sorting out wedding arrangements and working, as Dylan and Serena work so hard too, Jacqueline smiled back. Charlotte got up from her chair, "Thank you Jacqueline for a lovely afternoon, we must do this again sometime". "Yes, we must", as Jacqueline gave Charlotte a little hug. Charlotte was taken back but happy for it. Charlotte asked Jacqueline if she would like a lift back to her cottage, Jacqueline was only too happy to accept as she wanted to get home rather quickly as the need to call Serena was great indeed!

It was a sigh of relief! as Jacqueline's front door closed and she took a good breath! Jacqueline picked up the telephone to call Serena. The conversation was surprising to say the least on the part of Serena as she couldn't believe how Jacqueline had turned things around. "Oh, Jacqueline you are a gem an absolute gem", as Serena's face beamed on the other side of the telephone. Jacqueline persuaded Serena that there was no point in her coming along it was for the mother and the bride to be there. "I am sure it will work out fine! Phew! Jacqueline gasped at she put the receiver down". I think we have diverted a family crisis there, which need not be one. Charlotte and Serena never really fall out and it wasn't the time to do that… Jacqueline hummed away to the song from the radio, "You are my Sunshine", as hoovered the living room and cleaned the kitchen. Nothing like a good song to get the pulses racing, for hoovering was a chore, but it was a delightful one when it came to listening to a good song.

Serena and her mum, met in the car park at the Lake House. Charlotte was so taken back with the idyllic scenery, as she gasped at the shimmer of sunlight that floated over the lake, "Oh my, this is something else, Jacqueline was right". Serena looked overwhelmed by her mam's comments, as she thought the venue might not come up to Charlotte's high expectations. "It has a kind of supremacy about it, the way the deck to the lake adjoins the front entrance which is just set back enough so you can take in that glorious view of the lake; the beautiful landscape that surrounds it, I am most taken with the beautiful setting of how the water compliments the surrounding landscapes, that parallel contrast Serena"." Me too Mum, I couldn't put better myself, as you have eloquently sold it; you should take up sketching again

Mum as you have that eye for detail, "It's been a good while, I might just do that Serena", as they walked arm in arm through the front entrance. Mrs Beauchamp the venue organiser met them at the door to show them around.

As they walked on the beautiful marble floor towards the majestic high raised reception area, it looked like it had been manufactured out of a cosmopolitan magazine, its surrounding area with circular velvet seating, and the outlandish plants that stood so prominent make the reception area rather lavish with an inviting welcome. Serena was most impressed as was Charlotte as they made their way into the main hall. It's polished mahogany floor, such a total contrast from the reception area. It had that banquet medieval look about it, which Serena was looking for, Charlotte wasn't totally convinced, but Serena soon brought her around. The tables were so finely polished, obviously French polished by the look of things. There were several designs for the tables as Mrs Beauchamp pointed out the most favourable ones, Serena was taken with the white and pink lace designs as her bouquet was white and pink roses, and that was the one she was struck on. As they both stood back and viewed the room from different angles it was totally consuming with that heir of supremacy. "You were right mum it has that aura of supremacy", as they took one more glance at that glorious room and the glorious light that shone through the window with the view of the lake.

The conversation flowed over while they took a good turn around the lake. "I cannot wait for Dylan to come and look on Saturday, isn't it so romantic mam", "Yes, it is Serena, it certainly is". Mrs Beauchamp invited them to try out the food, and then they could all sit around the table and discuss whether they would like a buffet or a sit-down meal. As they sat and ate a variety of tasters, Serena was of the view that a buffet would be a great choice as the tasters were very appetizing, Vol-au-vents filled with every filling imaginable, from mushroom to salmon to pate. The canopies were also delicious. There would also be a hot tray for those who would like something hot, various meats and dumplings. Mrs Beauchamp mentioned that the Chef also does wedding cakes to order, Serena was exceedingly interested in that, as it was another one off her tick list.

Mrs Beauchamp went through the brochures, which were very extensive, lots of table designs to include different flower arranging and exquisite tree lamps of which Serena ticked that box for they were elegant and defined the table setting. All the boxes were ticked and smiles all around, Serena was completely ecstatic with the whole choice of designs.

The whole day couldn't have gone better, "Oh Mum, all we must do now is go and pick out my dress! And we can leave the cars to Dad, as you know he wants to contribute". "We can have a day out of town, I think we should go to York, beautiful wedding gowns in York Serena". "Ok mum, good idea".

As they headed home, Serena asked her mum to drop by at Jacqueline's as Serena was keen to show Jacqueline the brochures, as she had been most instrumental with the day's events and how fantastic they had turned out, Serena was eternally grateful to Jacqueline, they were becoming rather good pals.

As Charlotte pulled up at the cottage, she couldn't help but notice how quaint and beautiful the setting was, she imagined drawing this cottage, and would approach Jacqueline in conversation about it. They all sat in the garden and took in the view of the slithering waves that overlapped in the sea; they were in sequence like a regimental army taking control of the sea. "What a beautiful setting it is here that surrounds your cottage Jacqueline, "May I sketch it one day", "You are very welcome any time Charlotte, best make it soon before the season changes though, Autumn is just around the corner". "I will give you call next week, to arrange".

Serena could not help noticing how her mum had become alive again, as she hadn't done any sketching since she was young. Charlotte always said that she was too busy, but the real reason was that she had an accident with her left hand, where she had broken a finger, and it seemed to never mend properly. Charlotte became less and less confident about going back to drawing, as the time went by Charlotte filled her life around her husband and looking after Serena. After some time had passed Serena and her dad stopped prompting Charlotte to draw again. It was a great surprise to Serena to see her mum so animated, this day certainly has become a special day for all. "Oh, how dad will be so pleased about mum's escalation back to the drawing board", Serena thought to herself.

Charlotte was animated alright, but she was also terribly nervous about drawing again, she would do several drafts at home before coming over next week, that would give her plenty of time to prepare for the big day. It was if Charlotte had become reborn again, she felt this wonderful surge of energy and effectiveness and purpose that she felt was lacking in her life at this stage. Charlotte was ready for this new beginning.

As Jacqueline looked towards Serena and her mum, she thought how alike they looked in their stance and looks and how together they were. That is how a family should be. They drank lemonade and looked out at the seagulls as they all perched themselves upon Trow rocks, and the surfers had appeared to do their daily aerobics, it looked like there were plenty of newcomers today. There were two instructors down on the beach, it looked a party of beginners were arriving. "Oh, look Serena said, they have all come to have a beginners lesson by the look of it". Charlotte smiled and thought to herself, yes, they are starting something new, and how good it must feel, as I know how good I feel at this moment.

Chapter 21

It was Sara's first day at the hospital and what a busy day she had, no time to take in the induction, as they were short staffed, as she stepped into the deep end on the ward. The Matron was fully aware of Sara's experience, and she knew the patients would be in capable hands.

It was a general ward, where the patients were being assessed for their individual symptoms. Most patients seem to be suffering with broken bones, so most of them will go to the orthopaedic department. The minor injuries, Sara was more than capable of dealing with, and there were lots of them. The day seem to fly by so quickly.

Sara was asked to see Matron at the end of the shift, as she made her way down the long corridor towards Matron's office, she couldn't help but notice through the adjacent window that her cap had slipped slightly, "Ooh Matron won't like it", she thought, as she stood for a moment to get herself in shape. It must had been when I was doing that young boy's dressing on his leg, she muttered to herself before opening Matron's door.

"Come in Sara, have a seat, you have had a busy day, and I am very impressed with you, well done Girl", as Matron smiled at Sara. "I have thoroughly enjoyed it Matron". "If you have a minute, I will take your through our daily routine, and show you around before you leave". Sara was more than happy to be shown the ropes and to get to know where everything is, as it had been a mind-blowing experience for a first day!

John, Sara's husband had arrived to pick her up, Sara was dead on her feet, "All I want is a long a hot bath John", as she turned to her husband. "I bet sweetheart, hard day on the front line hey? You will get back into the swing of things again, if I know you", as he kissed Sara on the cheek.

"How was your day love?", I think our little venture to move here is starting to look quite lucrative, lots of orders. John owned a string of Stationery Stores, rather like a haberdashery store, which sold virtually everything, from stationery to porcelain ornaments, travel books, dictionaries, you name it John would buy it. He was looking to expand the Newcastle store to incorporate, ladies' perfumes, scarves, and gloves, maybe, it was another idea he had in his head. "Wow my husband! You have certainly been busy too by the looks of things". "We will fit right in here my love; it won't be long before our new home is ours". Sara got into the bath and soaked herself for a good hour, she was so relaxed. A good sit on the deck I think watch the waves go by and as the sunset goes down and reflect on the day. Sara was most happy with her day.

At the Gibson household, Dylan dropped Colm off and made his way over to Serena's to discuss the wedding plans, Dylan was just happy to go along with everything Serena wanted included his outfit, for he knew Sara had good taste. Serena wanted Navy Blue morning suits for the men as the bridesmaids would be wearing ice blue shimmer effect in their dresses, the background would be white and the ice shimmer would be floral throughout, which would have a curved design from the waist downwards, the upper part of the dress would a blue sash. Serena had thought of the design whilst window shopping in the crafts store in Newcastle. Anne the Dressmaker from Shields was well known in the town to be very precise and diligent with her handy work. Serena was more than happy with their meeting that took place some weeks ago.

As Dylan pulled up at Serena's Mr Inskip came out to greet him and they took a turn around the garden as he wanted to discuss something with Dylan, a proposition was in hand and Mr Inskip was hoping that Dylan could oblige. Mr Inskip sprung the idea of Dylan moving towards Alnwick once they were married. A barn conversion was going to be up for grabs in the spring, and Mr Inskip thought it an ideal property for the newly Weds, not to mention of course that it was closer to the Inskips. Dylan had never lived anywhere other than South Shields and was taken back by this proposition, not opposed, but taken back. "I will give it some thought Mr Inskip", Dylan replied looking a little shaken by the idea at this instance anyway.

They both went into the house to greet Serena and her mum. Serena took Dylan into the drawing room and Mr and Mrs Inksip left them alone to their own devices. As Serena chatted along about the venue. Dylan couldn't help but notice the sparkle in Serena beautiful brown eyes, he would do anything for her, even move wherever she wanted to live. As they discussed this barn conversion, Serena wasn't fully committed to it, as she wanted Dylan and herself to choose their new home, but they would both have a look at it to satisfy her dad's wishes.

It seemed as though Serena had fell in love with the Beach at South Shields, and they both had in mind to have a look at the properties along the coast road, as there were 3 up for sale, and in particular, there was , "The Gables", a very impressive house that stood back off Beach Lane which stood out from all the rest of them, its glorious wrought iron gates and featured garden at the front was a worth a look for that only. They would view the property that very weekend.

They all gathered for dinner, Serena avoided the subject of the barn conversion and kept the conversation on the Lake House which took up most of the night's conversation. Dylan was thankful for that, for Serena had a way with words, as she mentioned Jacqueline and how it all came about that The Lake House was the place to be, even her dad couldn't get over how Serena Sparkled when mentioning the whole day's events. "I shall have to come along and have a look at this infamous Lake House", as her dad chipped into the conversation. "You will be so impressed Dad", as Serena gave her dad a pleading look. "Next week, then, we shall have lunch there and look the place over". Everyone agreed, as Dylan gave an adoring look at his fiancée, "how lucky am I to have such a beautiful and intelligent love in my life", as he thought to himself...

The conversation turned to the ceremony, Serena glanced at Dylan, as their eyes met across the table, Dylan was the first to speak, "I will leave that to Serena, anything Serena decides I am happy with that". Serena's father was taken back with Dylan's comments, he thought Dylan would have had some input. Serena at this time was not sure how she felt about a Church ceremony, in her view she was hoping that The Lake House could accommodate them as there was a small Chapel at the rear of the property just on the outskirts of the Lake. Charlotte pitched in and said, "We can all have a look at the small Chapel next week maybe?". As Serena squeezed Dylan's hand under the table, "Yes, let's do that", as Dylan and Serena spoke simultaneously, it was as if they knew what one other were going to say. Charlotte laughed, "How unique, you both said that at the same time". They all laughed together.

Meanwhile Jacqueline was having a similar conversation with Declan, and Declan was so impressed with his wife and her handling of the situation; you have come into your own so masterful and confident my love, as he put his arms around her. "I am happy for our Dylan, he has come alive", as he went on to talk about Dylan, not only about his love life, but also his leadership at work, Colm has come on leaps and bounds, and Dylan has had a hand in it too.

Emily popped her head around the door, "Again ! aren't you two a little bit old for all this cuddling and kissing hey ", as Emily winked at them both. "I am going to give our Niamh a ring to catch up, I will leave you two love birds alone "… Declan and Jacqueline said, "Go on then off you go", as they snuggled up to each other on the sofa.

Emily was hoping Niamh was not busy as she was hoping to talk to her about Frankie. She was so eager to get her advice as Emily was the naïve one when it came to boys. Emily always kept herself to herself because of her early years of having asthma so severely, and now she is almost 20years old, the asthma seems to have subsided, and she was thankful for that.

As Emily dialled the number it rang out for some time and it was eventually picked up by a student in the dormitory, "Who do you want, what room number?". Emily paused, "Niamh Gibson, sorry I don't her room number?". "Hang on I will look on the board, won't be a tick", as she strolled back to the telephone, "Niamh is in 39, back end of the corridor, if you hang on, I will give her a knock". "Can I ask your name, you are being such a sport", "it's Clara, "thanks Clara".

Niamh eventually got to the phone, "Hey, big sis, how are you doing?". "I am doing good, I am going to a bistro in town on Friday with Louisa, we were there last week, and I met somebody". Niamh was so excited for her sister, "That's fantastic, who is he, I want to know everything". "His name is Frankie, but he is a bit sure of himself and you know me I am not that confident. "Oh, come on you are! really you are, it's because you don't go out that much and you just need to come out of yourself a bit, just be cool, you know how to be cool, I know how cool you can be, remember when we went exploring on the beach that night and you just went for it and jumped from one rock to the next, like a cool high jumper". "This is different, and you know it is", "It isn't Emily really it isn't you just need to believe in yourself. "Love you my Sis", "Love you more". "Get dressed up and go for it our Emily, I will call you on Saturday to find out how it went". "Ok, you always make me feel like I can do anything". "That's what sister's do, listen I going to have to go, queue is backing up now for the phone, bye for now".

Emily sat back in the chair, reflecting on her sister's advice, and recalled that night when she leaped over that rock, it was like a force of nature, yes, I was feeling exhilarated and confident, cool, as she smirked to herself... I am cool, I will keep saying that to myself.

As Colm swept in and messed Emily's hair, she hated that and gave if a smack on his arm, he laughed it off. "What you up to Sis". "I have just been talking our Niamh", "I hope she is doing good at that school of learning ", as he laughed and went into the Livingroom. Jacqueline and Declan were snuggled up listening to the radio, playing Frank Sinatra, "I've got you under my skin". "What this then mam, dad, aren't a bit old for this as Colm winked at them". Declan spoke up, "Wait until it's your turn lad", "Plenty time for that dad, Colm was more interesting in his sketches and going out with the boys.

Jacqueline got up and started to make the tea, "Glad you are doing that mam, I am starving". "You are always starving Colm, anybody would think I didn't feed you", as Jacqueline laughed entering the kitchen, she shouted through "Pork Chops, Roasties, veg, Yorkshires and trimming, mid-week roast". "Ah yes", love Pork Chops", as Colm winked at this dad. Colm was getting to be a strong strapping teenager.

As the Gibson's sat down to their mid-week treat, Jacqueline turned to Emily, "How is Niamh, she is doing good mam", "is that it, what did you talk about". Emily didn't want to get into that conversation with her mam, as the talk with Niamh was all about Emily and Frankie and Emily wasn't ready to talk to her mam about him, not yet anyways, so she just came up with a random chat. "Niamh is enjoying herself with her new friends and the Campus and Student Union is fab by all accounts. Emily couldn't believe she had just made this up, mind you, not quite as Niamh did say it was fab at the University. The conversation drifted towards Colm and Declan, as Colm's induction was over, and he would be entering into his 12-month apprenticeship as a junior draughtsman alongside his dad. Emily was pleased the conversation was taken over by the men of the house.

After the meal Emily made her excuses to leave the table by saying she needed to walk off that lovely meal, and it was still sunny so a long walk along the beach, across to the Trow rocks would do the trick. As Emily got to the Rocks, she sat and reminisced that moment of her leap of faith, "How the hell did I jump from that rock to the other?". It seems an age I go, well it was 5 years ago, as she laughed out loud. How she wished Niamh was here, how she missed her... Another Chapter, another beginning, how our lives change from one year to next, Emily sat for some time, just watching the waves go by, so serene, so

127

peaceful; the beach always gives you that inner self belief, she thought as she looked up to the sky, "I wonder why that is?" ... The tide was drawing in, time to head home.

Chapter 22

As Jacqueline drew the curtains on this misty Thursday morning she couldn't help but notice the leaves had all fallen off the trees as Autumn was upon us; the sea was changing, it was so misty like a glorious smoke screen that slithered across the sea, motionless, "Ooh what vision", Jacqueline soaked up the view of nature and its vibrant changes , she turned to Declan, "Time to get up love its 6.30am". The household was awakened, Emily was already up raring to go, Colm took a little longer always last up, always needed that little push out of bed, as he hid under the blankets, "No! it can't be already time to get up dad". "5 minutes lad or I will go without you". Colm knew when his dad spoke it was time to get up, and he did reluctantly. "I have got time for toast dad?". "Eat it in the car lad, we got an early start". Colm straggled out of the house, toast in his mouth, and his haversack half over his shoulder. His dad looked on with a curious look, "You need to pull your socks up lad, you are working lad now, no time to dither". Colm munched on his toast and muffled, "Yeah dad". "Don't eat with your mouth full is not a good look lad, mmm as Colm replied as he munched away.

Jacqueline quickly waved them off to work. It was her turn to get hurried as she herself was getting ready for a big day, Thursday had arrived and it was time to prepare for the Book Club, It was going to be a long meeting as they were discussing the novel, "Ruth". Everyone was going to be attending, Gloria, Patricia, Lydia, Joan, Polly, Lucy, and Christine. There were going to be two new members this week, Pamela, and Jennifer who were already familiar with the novel "Ruth", as they had both read it. "Let's hope Gloria and Patricia behave themselves today if that could be possible! Jacqueline muttered to herself, "I will eat my hat if that if that happened"

The walk along the Beach to the Church Centre was energetic as Jacqueline took her strides with purpose, but she couldn't surpass the misty morning that was so fluent, as she gazed at the sea, it's smouldering grey and quivering sounds that whistled up and down the beach.

Jacqueline was so grateful to Fr Donnelly who was kind enough to give up the back room in the Church Centre, as she entered the building Fr Donnelly approached her, "How are you Jacqueline, ready for your book club". "Yes Fr, it's going to be rather interesting because the novel we are discussing has many branches to it, let's see how it goes. "I will let you get on and will catch up with you later Jacqueline to see how it went". "Will do Fr, get the kettle on, I will need a cuppa after today". "My sentiments exactly", as Fr Donnelly gave a wry smile…

Gloria and Patricia were first to arrive, and the room was set for the rest of the group, as the rest of them strolled in like school kids entering the classroom. Gloria spoke first, by saying, "Can I go first this week Jacqueline, as I am in the seat that usually goes first?". Gloria made a point grabbing the seat as soon as she walked into the room, she was determined to be first. "Yes, of course, Gloria, as you are in the seat".

Gloria began first by pointing out that she thought the novel was depressing and showed Ruth to be naïve and taken advantage of. I thought Mrs Mason was a dragon, and I didn't like Mr Benson he was a nasty piece of work. I didn't finish it because I found it too dull. It was what Jacqueline had suspected and made a point of even if you don't like a novel you should persevere for you never know how the story is going to turn out and you might even change your mind, so please everyone read a novel fully before coming to the Book Club. Gloria gave Jacqueline a dismissive look as if to say, "Whatever", as she slumped into her chair and gave Patricia that curious look of dismay, as Gloria likes to have the upper hand, not this time though.

Patricia had read the whole novel, Gloria couldn't believe it as she slumped even further into her chair! Patricia began to give her opinion of the novel, by starting with Ruth. I found Ruth to be naïve at first, but I feel that as she grew as a person, she became strong and was in fact the heroine, who never gave up and sacrificed a lot for love. A heartbreaking story brought me to tears to be honest. The novel proves that women have more true grit than men in my view, Ruth proved that. Mr Bellingham was a weak man, and was ruled by his mother, and the ruling class. Everyone in the room listened tentatively awaiting their turn to speak and give their version of the novel.

Lydia began to say that she thought the author was portraying the class distinction by highlighting that women in service should know their place, but Ruth was different an illegitimate child who grew into a fine seamstress and took pride in her work, her main problem was being so naïve and ignorant when it came to the opposite sex. Jacqueline was so impressed with the enthusiasm from all, apart from Gloria of course.

Polly eager to give her version of events within the novel. I love the characters of the Bradshaw household. You have Mr Bradshaw the Solicitor, who takes in Ruth but changes his mind about her when he knows of her circumstances, he does not condone such a social behaviour, but must learn a lesson of morality and compassion when it turns out his son has no morals and embezzles money from the family firm. A family of double standards, it gives out the fact that class and money don't always give a man a good character. I feel the novel is saturated with diverse social conditions that surprise and shock the reader at times. Jacqueline was impressed with Polly's summary.

Jennifer had read the Novel from a spiritual perspective, as she felt that the author was construing the powerful essence of faith, for example Ruth, who is tortured by her sin, being an unmarried mother, but is always looking for atonement throughout the novel. Mr Benson the minister in the novel embodies that powerful growth of spiritual tone as they address human kindness by taking in Ruth and giving her a respectful place in the community, and Ruth in turn vows to live a spiritual life for her illegitimate son Leonard. Its powerful undertone when Ruth divulges her secret and his shunned by the residents.

Pamela spoke in a quiet manner, "You need to speak up Pamela", Gloria shouted out. Pamela was a little nervous and started to cough, she took a sip of water and dived into her summary, Pamela was an ardent reader and loved period novels. I think Mr Bellingham is a great character in the novel, he may come across as weak, but I believe he loved Ruth and if it were not due to the social conditioning and the class division between them both, as Mr Bellingham was an aristocrat and Ruth was a mere seamstress of no social standing or connections. Interestingly Mr Bellingham loses his social ranking and in fact changes his name to Donne to gain back his social standing in the community, not to mention securing his inheritance from a wealthy relative and becomes a member of Parliament". That is a good recollection of how the novel explores the social etiquette, and the problems that occur. We have time for one more speaker as the time is running out ladies.

Christine was interested in how ironic it was that Ruth meets up with Mr Donne (Bellingham) years later when she is employed as a Nurse and Mr Donne gets very sick and Ruth volunteers to nurse him and, in the process, she dies, and he lives. Ruth's courage and commitment to another human being goes beyond heroism. She becomes a spiritual figure, a likeness an Angel of Mercy. "That was nicely put Christine", as Jacqueline gave her a warm smile. Christine could have gone on a lot more about the spiritual aspect throughout the novel, but time had run out.

Well ladies that was most enjoyable and interesting from all of you, it was truly a magnificent novel of integrity, righteousness, and faithfulness, and lets us not forget about capitalism for which the author seems paramount on alliterating from time to time throughout the novel.

Everyone was quite exhausted with such a lot of discussion, "Oh it's definitely time for tea and biscuits, help yourself when you go through to the hall", as Jacqueline finished talking Gloria strolled across the room to her and looked mortified at such awful behaviour. "I must sincerely apologise Jacqueline, I found the debate today very moving, and everyone put so much effort into it and I just dismissed it as a bit of fun, I will do better next time, I promise". Jacqueline was astounded by Gloria's attitude how books and words can affect us in such a way she thought to herself as they moved into the hall.

Next time ladies we will do something lighter, how about some creative writing, let's all do a poem or a short story if you feel inclined, how does that sound. The interest was mixed so it was left for everyone sleep on it.

Jacqueline was exhausted and couldn't wait to get strolling on the Beach front, "I will take the short route and rest upon my favourite rock, how she loved Trow Rocks, and that beautiful connecting cove by that little stretch of sand, as she loved the view of Trow Rocks. It was a cloudy afternoon, and the sky was grey and waves in the sea seem to disperse like a folding concertina, "How delicate they look". as she gazed upon them.

The walk was slow but very soothing as Jacqueline approached the beach cove, she noticed a large object sticking out of the rock, it turned out to be a sketch book that had fallen off the rock and embedded itself between two rocks. As Jacqueline picked it up and opened it, there were drawings of ships and the lighthouse, and pier in the distance, these drawings were very good indeed, drawn with such a delicate hand Jacqueline thought to herself, as she browsed through them, she came upon a portrait of a young girl with long blonde hair carrying shells in her bucket. "I hope there is a name at the back of this book, please say there is a name at the back of this book". There was initials "BC" at the bottom of the page below the young girl's portrait, faintly, but nevertheless it was something to go by. "I must ask our Colm, he might know". Jaqueline briskly walked up to the cottage to start dinner.

Declan and Colm were first to arrive home after a day's work at the office, and along came Emily who was beaming, she couldn't wait to tell everyone that Belinda was a great window dresser and the wool shop looked like it had taken a step forward into the fashion world by all accounts. Jacqueline was so keen to have a look at it and it was decided that they would both go into together on Monday. Emily was not only beaming about the shop but her forthcoming night out with Lousia and the thought of bumping into Frankie gave her butterflies in her stomach.

Jacqueline brought the conversation around about the sketch book she had stumbled upon at the beach, Colm was stunned by the drawings and said, "Mam these are exceptionally good, it looks like someone knows what they are doing, BC? The only BC know is Ben Crumpton and it is not him Mam". Jacqueline decided to put a notice in the Post office and at the Church Centre to see if anyone may come forward. Colm was still browsing through the sketches and Jacqueline quietly steered them away from Colm. "Tea everyone, let's all sit around the table at one time if you please".

It would be another day before the author of such exquisite sketches was found, if ever they were??

Chapter 23

It was time, Emily began to scour through all her wardrobe in the hope of finding that perfect outfit; she was now onto the 10th outfit, swapping tops and slacks and then going onto dresses, mixing, and matching, Emily had her bed swamped with mixed outfits. "Right, that's it, I am making a meal of this too right I am! number 3 that's it that's the outfit. The black and white swing dress and her white boots. Niamh always said it looked the best on her, as she thought about Niamh so affectionately. Afterall, it goes with my hair up and the lovely head scarf that Niamh bought me for my birthday. As Emily swooped her hair up and tied the delicate scarf around her hair. Emily took one last look in the mirror and as she did her Mam popped her head around the door, "Ooh don't you look absolutely fabulous, it must be an important night for you to go to this much trouble?". "No mam, it's just Lousia and I, I just wanted to make an effort for a change". "Alright then pet, have a good time". Jacqueline was not convinced with that reply at all, she knew her daughter well. I hope he is a decent fellow… no doubt we will hear about him eventually.

Colm passed Emily on the stairs, "ow our Emily, don't you look amazing". "Thanks Col, Emily always called her brother, 'Col' to her mam's dismay. Declan was ready with the car to take Emily to the bistro, as she got into the car, Declan couldn't but notice how Emily had grown into a beautiful young woman, it was always Niamh who was the 'looker' of the family as she took after Jacqueline. Emily resembled her father's looks in some ways, as she had his stumpy nose and dibble in the chin. "Have a good night pet, and watch yourself, mind how you go". Emily could not help smiling at her dad as she kissed him on the cheek, "You always say that dad, and I always do". "Tara pet, see you later".

Louisia was waiting at the door of the bistro, "Ooh my! don't you scrub up nicely". "Oh, away with you, so do you mate". The

Bistro wasn't too crowded at this point as it was only 7pm and Emily and Lousia like to get in early to find their favourite stools which is set in the corner near the part of the little stage, in readiness for the entertainment that put on at 8pm. There was always a band or a solo singer on a Friday night. It was always best to get ahead because when the crowds arrive, they always make a dash near the stage. Emily's and Lousia's stools were fixed in the corner so no one could get in front or behind them.

As they ordered their drinks, Emily needed a Babycham as she was feeling nervous, and her stomach was doing summer salts, although she hid it well and looked as cool as a cucumber. Lousia was dressed in cream lace blouse and black slacks; she had an adventurous nature and wasn't too shy in saying what she thinks. "I hope Frankie brings his cheeky mate Ian with him tonight, or else I will be having a word with him mind". Emily tapped Louisa on the arm as if she was pushing her away, "Hey what was that for, as Lousia gave her devilish laugh", Louisa knew Emily was taken with Frankie, but she didn't want to push it, as Emily was a sensitive soul underneath, deep with it mind.

It was almost 8pm now and the Bistro was filling up nicely, as the Band tonight was, "Zantra", they were made up of two guitar players one on base, and there was a saxophone player at the back and a female singer Catrina. They were to come on at 8.30pm.

Frankie and Ian were in the bar just down the coast, "The Gray Hat". Frankie was well dressed tonight; he wore his best polo shirt dark tan colour and lightly tanned slacks; it had even been to the barbers that day to have a good haircut. His dark hair was swept back, he had a thick set of hair on his head, with a certain wave to it, and was glad of the haircut. As they both sat and drank their pints, Ian began the conversation by saying, "Let's hope Lousia is in tonight, I think she is a canny lass, great personality right up my street, and her mate looks a nice lass, don't you think Frankie?". "I do mate, let's hope the pair of them are in tonight, let's make away down there, the band should be coming on about now".

As they both arrived, they could hear the band playing out the 60s music, Junior Walker and the All Stars, "What does it take", you could hear the saxophone belting away, they were good alright. Frankie made his way to the bar, it was a hard task trying to get served as she shouldered his way to the side of the bar, and as he glanced sideways, he caught a glimpse of Emily, his stomach began to churn a bit, "Wow, doesn't she look amazing, maybe out of my league I think". Frankie eventually got served and managed to find a space to prop their drinks up. "The lasses are in Ian, in the corner". "Let's make our way over". "Not just yet Ian, let's just drink our pint and we can offer them a drink later". "What is wrong with you mate? shy or something, that's not like you at all, you usually just swoon in with your cheeky charm, has the lass got to then hey?". "Arrggh, shut up man! drink your pint before it gets warm.

Lousia had spotted Ian, and he caught her eye, and they both waved to each other. Louisa turned to Emily, "They are here Emily, wave to Frankie". Emily was reluctant at first but saw his eyes looking over and she gave a half wave back. The Boys made their way over to Emily and Lousia. Frankie was stunned by Emily's beauty and couldn't take his eyes off her, even Lousia noticed that. "How are you girls", Ian responded first. "We are good thanks as they both shouted out over the music". An hour had passed, and all their voices were strained, Frankie suggested that they walk along the beach front, to the "Gray Hat", as it would be quieter in there and there was seating outside which was rather like a conservatory style setting, and the view out to the sea was most appealing. Louisa energetically said yes straightaway, Emily nodded like a nervous child, although she never looked nervous on the outside.

They all strolled along the Beach front, Lousia took her place next to Ian, encouraging Emily to walk alongside Frankie. "It's a grand night isn't it", as Frankie turned to Emily. "Have you been out long tonight, Frankie?". "We had a pint in the Gray Hat earlier, it is our local actually".

Louisa and Ian were the first to arrive at the Gray Hat, as Frankie and Emily took a slow stroll and talked away. Emily got to know where Frankie lived, which was near the edge of the coast road, about 3 miles away. They talked about their professions; Frankie was impressed with Emily's enthusiasm regarding the Wool Shop. He couldn't help but notice how creative Emily was, as she explained the different wool yarns and blends that create different garments. "It must be interesting being a mechanic at a garage; you must get a lot of satisfaction from putting cars back together again I would think?", as Emily was trying to be that little bit knowledgeable; she hadn't got a clue really. Frankie explained that he had learned a lot from his apprenticeship year as he had a good teacher. "Come on you two dawdlers! some of us a dying for a drink like!" as Ian looked on exasperated!

There was a table overlooking the sea, Louisa grabbed it before anyone else did. The drinks were bought, and they all sat talking above one another. "Let's stick to one subject at a time shall we", as Louisa laughed aloud. Louisa was so chatty and cheeky with it, for she liked to devour the conversation completely! Frankie steered his seat slightly to the left and invited Emily to do the same so they could have a chat on their own. Louisia didn't even notice the effect as she was so busy talking about herself and Ian was encouraging her to do so, he loved her infectious smile.

Frankie moved the conversation to the cinema as he loved to go the cinema and see the latest movie that was showing. The new movie Airline was showing at the Alambra starring Burt Lacaster. Emily liked Burt Lacaster, so it was hit with her. Frankie suggested Saturday night, that was tomorrow, "Is that too soon for you, are you free?". Emily eagerly replied, "I would love to go tomorrow". Frankie was swooning with joy, "That's settled then, shall I pick you up from home?". "Yes, can do, what time?". "The movie starts at 8pm so pick you up at 7pm and we can have drink before we go in". "That sounds good". Louisa shouted over to them, "What are you so secretly talking about then?". "Ooh this and that", Emily replied. Frankie was surprised that Emily didn't tell Louisa about the cinema. Emily was quite aware that if Emily came along, she would talk all the way through the film. Frankie seemed to think that Emily wanted to be alone with him. The matter was put right when they both shared a taxi, Emily was quick to let Frankie know why she hadn't mentioned the cinema to Emily. Frankie was a little disappointed in Emily's explanation, but his respect from her had just gone up a notch or two, of which he found compelling.

As they pulled up outside Emily's home, Frankie took a quick look at the wonderful cottage, he turned his head to Emily kissed her on lips but didn't linger. "Until tomorrow". Emily was in a daze, she automatically said yes, bye". As Emily strayed towards the door, as she was in no hurry to go in as she watched the taxi go by and Frankie's head hanging out of the window waving away. The walk towards the front door took a while and Emily changed her mind and walked around the back and out the gate towards the Beach, it was cold as it was October, but Emily didn't feel cold at all as she sat on a pillar of Trow rocks and gazed at the stars and sea was loud, as the waves overturned in a furious manner. Emily at this moment felt as if the sea was talking to her, it was only the whistling of the waves and windy undertone. Her head scarf around her long hair was swaying in the wind back and forth. She didn't mind at all as she couldn't get Frankie out of her mind, that kiss stayed with her. "It must be because I have not been kissed that much, am I making too much of this?", as she talked to herself. A level head girl as she got up and muttered to herself turning towards home, she slapped her thigh, "Get a grip girl! starry eyed indeed", as she laughed entering the back door quietly as it was after midnight.

Jacqueline heard the door and came down the stairs, "your home, did you have a good night". "Yes, Mam I did", "And, anything to tell me? "Alright Mam, yes, Frankie will be picking me up tomorrow to go to the cinema, that should keep you happy now". Jacqueline smiled and hugged her daughter, it does, I am tired I am off to bed, me too Mam.

Emily couldn't sleep she tossed and turned the whole night, her feelings were mixed, happy one minute but cautious the next. She got out of bed a gazed out of the window for some time and concluded that steady is best and don't go rushing in. Cinema tomorrow and then date twice a week so as not to get too involved that was her game plan. Emily got into bed and sighed, sleep! I need my beauty sleep! Count the sheep or listen to the movement of the waves which were rather soothing. Emily gradually fell asleep...

Chapter 24

Frankie was in daze, not like him at all, as his friends always nicknamed him, 'Jack the lad'. Frankie was feeling way out of his comfort zone, as he awoke, looked at the clock 5am! You are kidding me! "What is happening to me! I don't wake up until 8 or 9pm!". He just couldn't get Emily out of his head, as he whistled away towards the bathroom, with a hop and skip, he was buzzing with excitement.

As the day took off, Niamh, was on her way home to see her family; she was eager to meet up with Emily as she wanted so to hear about her night out with Frankie, "I hope our Emily had a great night, and everything worked out for her", as she gave out a little sigh.

Jacqueline was up early, so too was Declan, they were both looking forward to seeing their daughter, it had been 3 weeks since Niamh left for university. Jacqueline turned to Declan, "Let's make this a great day, as I think Niamh is settling in really well at Dunston University and we better make the most of her when she comes home", "We will pet", as Declan put his arm around Jacqueline and squeezed her tiny waist. Colm was just Colm, acting as if it was a typical Saturday, "I don't know what the fuss is Mam, it's only our Niamh". Jacqueline turned to Colm, "You and your dry tone our Colm, nothing stirs you lad!". "You know me Mam, take everything with a pinch salt". "Aah well, lad, things can change, wait until you meet a lovely lass, then you might not be so laid-back lad". "Aye Mam if you say so as he slurped off shrugging his shoulders.

Niamh arrived home with a warm welcome, she felt overwhelmed now as she hugged and kissed her Mam and Dad. "Let's get you in lass, you are looking really well", as her Mam grabbed her face and kissed her cheek. Declan noticed how his little girl had turned into a beautiful young lady. They all sat around the kitchen table, "Where is Emily Mam?", as Niamh looked confused. Jacqueline turned to Niamh, "Emily was late getting in and think she had woken about half an hour ago, she is probably in the bathroom, leave for a bit, tells us all about your weeks at Dunston". "Mam, Dad, the campus is amazing, I am having the best time, so happy Jess and Kate are with me too. We have had some fun at the Student Union, the bands that play there are so good... The lectures are so compelling, I am loving Austin, Bronte, and my favourites the Romantic Poets, Shakespeare too. There is so much to do, as the essays you must write are so much longer than college, so I am getting to grips with structure and how to conquer my hypothesis and getting it right in the first paragraph of my essays. Your argument must be convincing to get a good mark. Jacqueline was focused on Niamh, "Sounds very academic". "It is Mam and I have to work hard I know that". Declan smiled, "You will pet, you always give your best". Colm looked bemused, "It all sounds a bit too complicated if you ask me ". Declan slapped his head, "Nobody is asking you lad ", as they laughed away. "I am going to Emily now Mam, as Niamh hurried up the stairs.

Niamh entered the bedroom, Emily was at the dressing table drying her hair, as she turned around Niamh gripped her with a tight hug, "Ooh you are squeezing me to hard our Niamh, come on let's sit on the bed and have a good catch up". Emily began energetically, as they both crossed their legs turned to each other. "I don't know where to begin our Niamh". "Just take your time, from the beginning". Lousia and I got the Bistro as usual in our usual places, the place was heaving by 8pm. Frankie and Ian arrive just after 8pm and I had such butterflies our Niamh, Louisa, you know Louisa, she had to wave and get them to come over. Everything just moved so quickly I think one minute we were in the bistro and next we were strolling along the coast road, to the "Gray Hat". I suppose if the music hadn't been so loud then Frankie and I wouldn't have strolled so slowly to the "Gray Hat". We just seem to click instantly; I find it rather strange at the min. Oh! Our Niamh, you know me, so well contained usually and I am out of my comfort zone. You are not going to believe this, but I said yes to going to the cinema tonight, we are going on our own! "Wow! Emily, I cannot believe it, he must be special that's for sure. He is going to be picking me up here at 7pm. "Ah well, that's it then I am staying the night here at home, I was going to head back after tea, but I am not now. "You cannot do that Niamh! What about your night out with Kate and Jess". "I can see them anytime, anyway, I think Mam and Dad would love me to stay tonight, I am quite looking forward to it now, I will telephone them in a bit to let them know, what are you going to wear tonight?".

As they both headed to the wardrobe and got every item of clothing out to the bed, "Let's see what we can mix and match with this lot". "You could borrow my blouse; you so love Emily". Niamh's blouse was a chiffon pale blue with two toned colours, with a frill around the collar and down the buttons, and on the bottom of the sleeves, it was stylish blouse. "All we need now is a lovely pair navy slacks to with them and your ballerina navy shoes, and that pale blue scarf for your lovely long hair, let's dress you". They laughed and giggled and when Niamh had finished dressing Emily, they both looked into the mirror and Niamh said, "Frankie is going to be so impressed with you, not that he isn't already". Jacqueline popped her head in, "What is going on in here then", as she moved towards Emily, don't you look very stylish, I take it this is for the cinema tonight?". Emily beamed with admiration for Niamh as she looked at herself in the mirror. "I do look rather good don't' I", as she turned and gave a loving look at Niamh. "It's one o'clock man, time to get your jeans on and have some lunch Emily, plenty of time to get glammed up later.

Emily and Niamh headed to the kitchen where lunch was served, Jacqueline had put quite a spread on for Niamh's homecoming weekend, there was enough food to feed an army. "I am glad you have made so much food mam, as I am staying until tomorrow, just thought you should know, so plenty of food for later too", as Niamh tucked into the homemade mince and onion pie. Jacqueline gave a brief glance at Declan with joyous chin, "Oh so we have to put up with you for a weekend do we", as Jacqueline jokingly teased Niamh as she squeezed her hand. Colm was too busy to notice as he was well into the food. Emily wasn't that hungry as she had other things on her mind, her thoughts kept drifting back to Frankie, as she vaguely entered the zestful conversation between Jacqueline, Declan, and Niamh. Emily was happy to sit in the background and listen to Niamh describing her 3 weeks at university. Jacqueline and Declan were pleased if not relieved that Niamh was already making her mark at university at this early stage in her degree.

It was almost time for Emily to get herself ready for Frankie arriving, "I thought you were leaving at 7pm, it's only 5.30pm", as Jacqueline turned to Emily with a bemused look on her face. "It will take me at least an hour mam to get ready, my hair and makeup and finishing touches mam". Emily gave her mam a curious look and Jacqueline responded by saying, finishing touches, whatever is that you are saying?". "I will do the finishing touches, in getting your hair right". Niamh entered in the conversation. "Oh, I see your personal dresser", as Jacqueline laughed towards Delcan. Emily and Niamh chuckled away and swiftly climbed the stairs to the bedroom.

Frankie had his own agenda and made a purchase of a new pair of slacks and a top of range checked shirt, a Ben Sherman shirt from the high street. He was on his way after having a very busy afternoon valeting and washing his Hillman Imp motor car. He nervously went up the path of the cottage and took a long gaze at the sea, "What a spot, what a place to have a home, I am going to have a place by the sea one day, he gathered his thoughts and rang the bell, not before brushing his black hair back.

Declan answered the door, "Hello Frankie, step in for a minute she is just about ready". "Thank you, Mr Gibson,", Frankie replied. "Just call me Declan Frankie, no formalities in this house lad". Frankie was relieved to hear that. As Jacqueline got up to say hello, she was taken back by his well-dressed attire, very well dressed she thought, he has gone out of his way to make an impression, she liked that about him. Frankie said Hello to Niamh with a half a smile, as he was still in that nervous mode. Niamh couldn't help but notice that he was a handsome lad, just as Emily as described him, he better not break her heart or else he will have me to answer to, as she shook his hand.

Emily entered the room and Frankie eyes looked like they were going to pop out of his head, he spontaneously said, "Emily you look stunning", he couldn't hold it back. "Aw thank you Frankie, shall we go now". They both left the house and as they all stood at the door, Niamh turned to her mam, "They look so good together, mam, he better not hurt her, or else". Jacqueline put her hand on Niamh's shoulder, "something tells me he is smitten to the core; I don't think he will". They all went into the living room and Declan started to say, "Our Emily has started to shine, and it showed tonight". Colm by this point was out the back door to meet up with Tom and his mates for a game of footie.

Sara and John had popped in as they had just been walking their Dog Brodie, a cocker spaniel along the beach. "Aw our Sara you have just missed our Emily going out with her new boyfriend Frankie". Aw never mind I am sure we will meet another time. "How is the job this week, are you settled in properly now at the hospital Sara?". "I am, yes, it's wonderful, I feel like I have been there for years". Everything couldn't be better, we have started to re-decorate the beach house and plan to have an extension on the front, more space for our Brodie to linger about in. "That sounds good", as Delcan entered the conversation.

It was declared that they would all play a game of trivia and Niamh was more than up for that, music later and some dancing I think as Declan planned the evening ahead. Niamh was glad that she had was staying the weekend and wasn't that bothered about her personal life as she was focused on her studies and wasn't going to get attached and planned to just have acquaintances throughout her time at university. The Trivia game was going well for Niamh as she was beating everyone hands down, "I win again, another matchstick to me, they played for matchsticks in place of money; that's ten matchsticks altogether", as she jumped up and down.

Declan got up, "That's it now, music time". "I get to pick all the music as I am the winner", as Niamh hurriedly jumped towards the radiogram, the Four tops, 'I will there' was first up, followed by the Temptations and Al Greene, even John got up with a lot of persuasion from Sara. They all danced away until midnight....

Chapter 25

Frankie and Emily had arrived at the cinema. Frankie was hesitant in being seated at the back so chose to be seated 4 rows down, he wasn't prepared to make a move on Emily not in the first date, even though he was dying to kiss her. Emily was surprised he had chosen to sit further down the row; she liked him even more for that.

As they left the cinema holding hands, Frankie turned to Emily, "Did you like the movie?", "Oh yes, it was exciting, so glad they saved so many on the aeroplane. They both strolled along the street and Frankie asked if Emily was hungry as they passed by the fish and chips, "Oh yes, let's have some fish and chips", as Emily smiled at Frankie. They strolled towards the beach and sat on the edge of the wall and looked over to the sea. "Thank you for a lovely night Frankie", "I hope we are going to have a lot more nights like this, aren't we?". "Yes Frankie, we are". Frankie put his fish and chips down and put his hands gently around Emily's face and kissed her passionately, she could hardly breathe, he had in fact taken her breath away. They sat for some time, Emily eventually looked at her watch and found it was passed mid-night, she was getting cold, and Frankie put his jacket around her shoulders. "Shall we make tracks Frankie, the wind his getting chilly". Frankie was reluctant to move but felt he should as he didn't want to spoil such a perfect night. They made their way to Frankie's car.

Emily arrived home and had planned to meet up with Frankie the following Wednesday, they were going to the "Gray Hat" for the quiz night. As Emily put the key in the door, Niamh came down the stairs, "Ooh you stop out! it almost 1am, mam and dad went to bed ages ago, let's have a cuppa and you can tell me about your date. Niamh could see from Emily's face as she talked and talked that her sister was smitten so smitten. Niamh told Emily to keep her head and not to go too fast with her new romance, just keep a level head our Emily. They hugged and yawned and made their way to bed.

Sunday Morning was upon us, and Jacqueline had gone to Mass, the girls were fast asleep. Colm and Delcan went off for the morning football down at the local field, Colm was playing and Dylan was on his way. The telephone rang and rang and eventually Niamh slowly came down the stairs with her eyes half open, yawning, "Ooh who is this! Hello, Niamh it's Jess, when you are coming back! we need you!", "Why what's happen?". "You missed a great night; Andrew was gutted you weren't there; I had a ball with Ben he is so funny". Kate, needed you, as she wasn't overall keen with James, she finds him too full of himself. "Niamh laughed down the telephone, chill Jess, I am coming back this afternoon, you can tell me everything". "You sound tired Niamh, sounds like you had good night". "Yes, I have enjoyed my family get together, we had a party last night it was great". "Ok party girl, we will see you this after, bye for now".

Jacqueline's morning had turned out to be unexpected as she has had a response from the notice she had put out in connection with the missing sketchbook, Jacqueline had completely forgotten about it as it had been a few weeks. There was telephone number and a name, Bernadette Crams, "Ooh just to look at that we have success at last, it's been weeks", as Jacqueline turned to Fr Donnelly. "What's this then Jacueline?", Fr replied. "It's a sketchbook with wonderful sketches I found on the beach weeks ago, our Colm demanded that I seek the owner out, so I put a Notice here at the Centre. and in the Newsagents shop. "That is good news, good for Colm, they must be great sketches for Colm to make a fuss as he has a good eye for anything artful". "It certainly does Father".

Jacqueline made her way home as she was eager to catch up with Bernadette Cram, Jacueline's journey along the beach as she was heading near home she was interrupted by a young girl with light hair, blue eyes and a slim build came upon her. "Excuse me I have just come from the Community Centre; you don't happen to be Jacqueline Gibson at all?". "I am", as Jaqueline looked on with a confused look on her face. "My name is Bernadette Cram, and I am the owner of the sketchbook, they told me at the Community Centre that it was a Jacqueline Gibson who was in possession of my sketchbook. I telephoned your home as they were kind enough to allow me access to your telephone. "What a coincidence, I was just eagerly walking home to telephone you; we can walk together, and you are welcome to stop for a coffee if you have time. Bernadette looked at Jacqueline in surprise, "Yes, I would like that, thank you".

They both entered the cottage and Jacqueline put the kettle on, "Take a seat Bernadette, I will fetch your sketches". Bernadette got quite emotional as her sketches meant so much to her, there were sketches of her father in her folder, who had recently passed away. She was at the beach near Trow Rocks that day because it was the last time, she saw her father alive; it was their favourite spot where her father always took her as a little girl where she would ride on the shuggy boats and collect cockles and shells. Jacqueline slumped back in her chair! "Trow Rocks is our favourite spot too, I suppose there are many out there who think the same, but what a coincidence, you could say fate even. Bernadette nervously smiled back at Jacqueline; her eyes were rather watery at this point.

On that day she misplaced her sketchbook folder, Bernadette had spotted a young girl on the donkey ride, and she was so distracted as she put her sketchbook folder down and it slid down the rock. It reminded her of her father, and she got up so quickly and gathered her things and had not really noticed anything missing until she arrived home.

Jacqueline came in the with the coffee and was taken back by Bernadette's distress, she thought she would be so happy. Bernadette began to tell her story to Jacqueline, Jacqueline was so moved by it and couldn't help but notice this lovely young girl 16 years old, looking so lost. Bernadette was so close to her father and her mother was stricken with grief, she felt so isolated and the only thing that comforted her was her sketchbook. Bernadette couldn't thank Jacqueline enough. They talked on about

149

Bernadette's talent and Jacqueline enquired if she was enjoying Art College, it seemed now when Jacqueline started to talk about Art, Bernadette's face lit up and she felt alive now, she hadn't felt like that for weeks. The conversation drifted on and on for some hours, as they had covered every aspect of famous artists, such as Turner, Constable, Monet, Mane, Van Gogh, and her favourite Renoir.

Colm and Declan had arrived home for tea, Jacqueline had completely lost time, as she introduced Bernadette to Colm and Declan. Colm's face lit up like the fireplace, it had always wondered who was behind those fabulous drawings. "Would you like to stay for tea Bernadette?". Yes, I would, can I call my mam to let her know if that's ok". "Of course, you can". Bernadette called the house, and Jake her brother answered, he answered in his muttered tone, and just said, Aye, our Bernadette, see you later". Jake was 12 years old, and he is a great comfort to his mam.

Colm hurried upstairs to get changed, he put on his favourite casual shirt and black slacks. Declan was aware his son seemed rather enthusiastic with his approach to his attire, he usually got changed into his track suit, he was never out of his track suits, except on special occasions, I wonder what brought his transformation about?... Colm came briskly into the dining room where Bernadette was sat browsing tenderly through her sketchbook. "I think your sketches are amazing Bernadette, may I select some I particular thought were awe inspiring". Bernadette gazed at Colm and gasped with amazement. Colm pointed out the sketches of the shuggy boats and how Bernadette had captured the length of beach which had a great view of the lighthouse, Bernadette was extremely descriptive with her perspectives to create dramatic imagery, Colm was fascinated. Bernadette was delighted with Colm's response, and they spent some time in detail with various sketches, such as, the Trow rocky coves which stood out magnificently. Colm couldn't believe such talent, "I bet you will end up being an Architect of designer that's for sure". Bernadette responded by saying that she was so interested in being a designer but wasn't sure what path

150

to take yet, she felt it would become clear when she finished college.

Tea was on the table, and they all enjoyed that chicken casserole of which Jacqueline luckily just had to heat up. Declan began a conversation to find out more about Bernadette and her family and where she lived. Jacqueline intervened and said, "Not just now Declan". "It's fine Mrs Gibson, my dad passed away a few weeks ago with a sudden heart attack, and I live at home with mam and brother Jake who is 12 years old, we live in Berton End Park just off the coast road in a semi-detached 2 bedroom. "I am so sorry for your loss Bernadette, I only asked where you lived so we could offer you a lift home ". "Thank you, Mr Gibson, now dad is passed there is no one to drive the car, but I am hoping to take lessons next year". "Then that's settled Bernadette no rush, you can stay for some dessert at least, its strawberry trifle". Bernadette stayed on for another hour and Colm was delighted, he insisted on accompanying his dad in the car. Bernadette sat in the back while Declan insisted Colm sit in the front, "Let the girl breathe, Declan whispered to Colm".

It was 7-minute drive which nothing at all, and Colm got out of the car and walked to the pavement and boldly asked Bernadette if she would like to go sketching at the Beach on Sunday. Bernadette was pleased Colm had asked such a question, as she felt like she was back to normality at least for that space of time, it elevated Bernadette and she wanted to feel elevated once more.

Bernadette entered the living room where her mam and brother were sitting watching tv, a quiz show was just starting. Lena her mam asked if she had a nice time and was so pleased that Bernadette had recovered her sketchbook as she knew how much it meant to her. Bernadette was too dazed to sit and watch tv and made her way upstairs with the excuse of having to prepare a piece for college. In fact, Bernadette just sat on her bed and looked out of the window and gazed in a trance for the next hour, her thoughts were on how animated the Gibson family are and how Colm's view on art captivated her attention and it seems that attention was taking up a lot of her thoughts. Bernadette's thoughts were how she could expand her perspectives on her next piece, she was so looking forward to Sunday and what it had in store.

Colm was of the view that Bernadette was an exceptional girl, and she wasn't too bad looking at all. For the first time Colm has shown an interest in a girl, Declan and Jacqueline were dumfounded, our Colm who only looked at a girl and would say, "Cackling hens are girls, always giggling, not for me mam". Declan and Jacqueline were now aware that their son has is now growing up at 17years old, he chatted on about Bernadette's sketches, Jacqueline couldn't shut him up. "Our Colm you are sounding like right old chatterbox, if I didn't know any different, I would say that you are right taken with Bernadette". "Arggh come on mam, I like her drawings a lot and yes, we are going to draw together at the beach on Sunday, that's all mam, don't get carried away mind". Jacqueline gave him a smug look and winked at Declan.

"I am off to see Tom, get some footie practice in for Saturday". "Aren't you forgetting something lad, you need to change into your tracksuit for that lad", Declan smirked at Colm. Colm had completely forgotten about that his mind was elsewhere. Jacqueline turned to Declan, not taken by Bernadette, I will eat my hat, as Declan and Jacqueline hugged and laughed at each other.

Chapter 26

Emily had arrived home from a late shift at the shop, as the new stock had arrived and there was the new window display to set up, Belinda kindly stayed behind to assist Emily. Aileen had also called in and noticed how extremely busy they were, and it was thought that another part time assistant wouldn't go a miss in the shop, Emily was relieved to hear that. Aileen would advertise that very week, and insisted on driving Emily home as she was hoping for a catch up with her sister Jacqueline, it seemed an age since they had a good chat. As they chatted away on their way home, Aileen suggested to Emily that she might consider taking over the shop completely in the future. "Aunt Aileen, I couldn't possibly afford to take it over completely, but it is a nice offer". "I think you should think about it not just yet, but in the next few years, it will be good for you, as you love it so much". Emily dreamed of it so many times, but the reality she thought was way out of her reach. Emily had no idea that her Aunt Aileen had other plans but did not want to make them known as this stage. Aileen's idea was to present it to Emily on her 21st birthday, which would be next year. Emily had worked so hard to make the Wool Shop the success it is, and Aileen was so impressed with the profits and how Emily became so constructive and so creative. It was Aileen's plan, and she was going to stick with it.

As Aileen pulled up to the cottage, Jacqueline was so happy to see her sister as it had been too long. They gathered in the dining room and sat for hours while Jacqueline divulged all the happenings in the Gibson household. Jacqueline began to tell the story of the missing sketchbook, and how Colm reacted to it. Aileen was not surprised to hear about Colm as he is an amateur painter by nature since he was 5 years old. "He may have found his soulmate our Jacqueline". "I think you might be right there our Aileen", as they laughed and sipped tea and homemade scones. Aileen loved Jacqueline baking and cooking and was rather envious that she wasn't such a dab hand at it. Jacqueline was the one who spent most of the time with their mam in the kitchen, Aileen was interested in knitting and sewing, baking, and cooking was not her favourite past time, she just loved to eat when their mam put it on the table.

The conversation turned to Emily and her dates with Frankie. Aileen looked surprised as she turned to Jacqueline, "Emily never mentioned it, mind you we were so engrossed in conversation about the shop and a new assistant". Aileen however was delighted for Emily. "It's about time Jacqueline, she does work so hard and it's just what she needs I am sure". "It's the first time I have ever seen her light up like a Christmas Tree, you should have seen her when Frankie called for her, she was glowing". "Let's hope it stays like that our Jaqueline". "Early days yet, so glad she is enjoying herself so much". "How's Niamh is she doing alright". "Our Niamh was here this last weekend; she is loving it". "Aww that great our Jacqueline, I knew she would, I knew she would take to it like a duck to water".

This has been a great catch up our Jacqueline, let's do lunch next week, I will take you into town at Maskies for lunch. "Maskies! Our Aileen that's a bit pricey!" "I can spoil my sister if I want to, so that's settled for next Wednesday". They both hugged each other tightly and pecked each other on the cheek.

Jacqueline tidied up and couldn't help thinking about Niamh, I wonder if she will come home again so soon as it was such a good weekend, having her here for 2 days. Jacqueline sighed and got the vegetables and potatoes out in readiness for tea and the men of the house coming home.

Dylan accompanied Declan and Colm home, as his car was in the garage for service. Jacqueline had made extra vegetables and potatoes on, there was plenty of mince and onions to go round for all. I am so glad you could join us Dylan, it's been a while, how are the wedding plans going?". Dylan tilted his head, "Well, they seem to be going ok, but the main problem I think what we will come up. against is the ceremony". "Why is that Dylan", as Jacqueline looked over to him with a confused look. "Serena's mam seems to favour a registry type service which can be conducted at the Lakeside, as they have that small chapel like building at the back, but Serena is torn, I get the impression she would like a priest to preside, I am convinced that me being Catholic has thrown Serena, and she is a big fan of yours Jacqueline". "I hope it has not caused any confrontations with her parents, as I would hate to be the culprit". "I don't think it has as yet, but you know Serena when she has a bee in her bonnet she never let's go". "Maybe I could have a word with Fr Donnelly and see if he could give a blessing at the Lakeside after your service". "Let's just see how things pan out, as we do have 6 months to decide. I will be the peacemaker", as Dylan laughed it off.

Declan looked rather tired, and a little pale, Jacqueline looked her husband and said, "You ok love", as Jacqueline looked a little concerned. "It's just a bit of headache that's all, I will take a paracetamol love". Dylan looked at his brother and yes, he said, "You do look pasty our Declan". "I am alright, apart from this bloody headache". Colm put his hand on his dad's shoulder and said, "Dad you had some tablets early on". "I think I might be coming down with cold son, that's what it is, let's just eat, I am starving". Declan knew he was lying at little, this headache was no headache, it was persistent today, other days it was just on and off. He was convinced it would pass, a virus, is coming he was sure that of that.

As they all sat around the table, Emily asked if she could be excused as she was going out that night with Frankie, they were to meet up with Louisa and Ian at the 'Gray Hat', it was quiz night, Frankie loved Quiz night, it amused him so to see others get so competitive and bad tempered if they didn't win, it was fun watching them all.

Emily hurried upstairs and put on her casual jeans and top with her ballet shoes, and Frankie called for her at 6.30pm as the quiz was starting at 7pm. Dylan was introduced to Frankie and was most impressed with his manners and his eye for fashion. "He is a smart lad, I will give him that", as he smiled at his brother Declan. "You better get yourself to bed brother with a hot toddy in my opinion". "I will, bro, it will pass", as they all said their goodbyes to Dylan.

Declan made up a hot toddy and sat a while watching the news on the TV, while Jacqueline looked with a worried look on her face. Colm sat with his mam and said, "He is ok mam it's just a headache and cold coming on, do need to get het up mam". "You probably right son; you know me worry about anything". Declan went to bed, he started to sneeze, and the cold was showing its face. Colm and his mam sat and watched TV, "The Morecambe and Wise Show is on in a bit, shall we watch it our Colm". "I am off out mam, it's footie practice, remember". Jacqueline had completely forgotten, she was still thinking about Declan, "I will go up in a bit and check on him".

Declan was coughing and spluttering and soon went off into a deep sleep, that hot toddy had done its business. Jacqueline couldn't concentrate on TV and turned it off, as she entered the bedroom, she could see Declan was fast asleep, she picked up a handkerchief and wiped his forehead, it was very sweaty, the hot toddy was bringing out the cold in him. Jacqueline at this point felt relieved as she always felt that every time Declan had a headache it reminded her of the mining accident and his head surgery and the fact that he still had to have 12 monthly check-ups at the hospital. Jacqueline slept in Niamh's bed to let Declan rest.

Jacqueline's thoughts turned to the mining accident and its devastation, "Thank goodness everyone came together, and life seems to be getting back to normal until something hits you and reminds you", as she muttered to herself.

The next morning Declan awoke feeling so much better, Jacqueline tried to persuade him to stay home, she knew she would fail, as Declan had never missed work, except for his time in hospital and recuperation at home. "There is no point me making a fuss then", as Jacqueline put her arm around Declan. "No, my pet, I am fine, Beecham Powders in my jacket". He kissed Jacqueline on the cheek, "no proper kiss pet, keep my germs to myself", as he left house smiling, Colm following on as usual with his toast in his mouth, always last out.

Emily was pushed for time too this morning, as she had a late night, it turned out to be hilarious as the quiz night turned rather sour as the red team weren't convinced they hadn't won, even Emily was amused by their antics shouted and screaming , "That's our prize money", all for a few bob, Emily was still smiling about it, as she was telling her mam, her mam was in stitches, grown men squabbling over a quiz and a few bob what is world coming to.

Jacqueline gathered the dishes up and headed to the kitchen when the telephone rang, it was Serena asking if Jacqueline was free at lunch time, "Yes, I am Serena, shall make a sandwich for you". "Aw no bother Jacqueline, I will get us a deluxe sandwich from the restaurant, my treat". "Ok Serena, see you at 1pm", as Jacqueline put the telephone down, thinking out loud whilst watching the breakfast dishes, "I know why she is coming, I must be tactful, and not sway Serena into something she may regret, on the other hand, it is Serena's decision, I will let her do the talking, that is it, that's a good plan.

Lunchtime arrived, Serena pulled up in her mini cooper car, it was rather stylish, as Serena was nothing but stylish. Jacqueline greeted Serena with a friendly hug and kiss on the cheek. "You are looking well Jacqueline", "So are you, always looking fabulous". "Aww you are a spoiler", as she put the sandwich boxes on the table. "What do we have here then". I thought you would like a box with everything sort like a ploughman's lunch; the restaurant across the street from the office prides itself on homemade, so let's see if it lives up to its reputation". There was everything in cheese, ham, pickles, side potato salads, homemade pork pies, a lovely piece of mango chutney on the side. "Wow, this is a mouthful isn't it, thank you pet, it's gorgeous". "Aww your welcome".

I came today to pick your brains on the service for the wedding, I am torn between a proper church wedding, instead of having the registry type service at the chapel building behind the Lakeside, I am just drawn to having a priest there to make it more traditional, Mum thinks the style of the registry at the Lakehouse is quite fitting, it's lavish, the organisers talked us through it, but I am not convinced. Jacqueline put her hand on Serena's arm and said, "You and Dylan are the ones to sort this one, it's down to how comfortable you feel in the surroundings, are you comfortable being a Church of England is that it?". "Oh yes, I am, it's not that, it's just having a priest there would make me feel more comfortable as I feel traditional is for me". "Ok then Serena, I could have a word with Fr Donnelly and see if he could bless your wedding at the Lakehouse, you could still have it at the Lake House, registry style, but have a blessing afterwards, I can only ask him, it not out of the question I am sure, as Fr Donnelly is obliging, loves to help people in a dilemma". "Aww Jacqueline, that sounds terrific it really does, just let me know what he says". Serena went back to work a very happy young lady.

Chapter 27

Colm and Declan arrived at the office, Colm couldn't help but notice his dad didn't look at all well, and he was trying in vain to get his dad to turn back and go home, Declan looked up at his son Colm, "It's just a cold lad, you cannot miss work just for cold, remember that when we get a cold". Colm looked towards his dad as they entered the main office and wasn't convinced that his dad just had a cold, he looked too pale and clammy to the touch as Colm had grabbed his dad's wrist when they got out of the car.

The morning went by quickly as it was the busiest period in the office with drawings and specs to be done for the engineers to crack on with their workload which was mounting up somewhat. Declan's headache wasn't going away even with the painkillers, as Declan turned to the photocopier machine, he went down with a thud, and then knocked his head against the corner of the copier, he was out cold. Melvin the First Aid attendant in the office rushed over the Declan who was not breathing, he had no pulse and there were no vital signs at all. Melvin had taken the CPR course, so he went straight into action, and in the meantime, Colm rushed to telephone the emergency services. Melvin was not getting any response from the CPR! he checked his vital signs and still no input, Melvin continued with the CPR for 15 minutes; the paramedics had arrived and took over with shock pads to try and restart his heart, still no response, there was nothing anyone could have done more for Declan had gone! The office was at a standstill, no one could move they just all stared at each other in shock, Colm was inconsolable, he couldn't let go of his dad. The Managing Director telephoned Dylan who was in the engineering room on the Anszac Ship which was docked nearby.

Dylan ran into the office went down on his knees to his brother, the paramedic turned to him and said, "I am sorry for your loss". Dylan held his hands in his head, "What the hell happened here!" tell me! what has happened! He yelled and yelled, someone! give me the answers! The senior paramedic explained that Declan's body would have to be taken to the mortuary and examined to find out the cause of death. Dylan wanted the answers and asked how long that would take, he wanted to know asap what had happened to his brother. The Senior paramedic notified Dylan that it would take at least a few days to give any kind of indication as to the cause of death. Dylan looked disgusted at the answer and turned to Colm and put him his arms around him and cradled him for what seemed like hours. Declan's body was taken away and Colm and Dylan left the office to make the journey home and let Jacqueline know the devastating news. "What I am going to say to Jacqueline! how can get the words out! as Dylan muttered to himself, Colm just couldn't control his tears, it was too much for him. Dylan was determined he would keep together until he was alone with his own thoughts.

Colm ran into the cottage, Jacqueline was upstairs changing the beds, she wasn't expecting anyone and when she heard Colm shouting mam! she hurried down the stairs, "What on earth Colm! Why are you crying son! Whatever is the matter!". Dylan entered the room put his arms around Jacqueline and hugged her tight, as she released herself, she said, "Where is Declan! why are you looking at me like that!". Dylan tried in vain to get Jacqueline to sit down but she was not having that, she began to yell, please! tell me! Where is my Declan! Dylan began trying to explain to Jacqueline what had happened, Jacqueline couldn't take anything in what Dylan was saying it was as if someone had put muffs on her ears, she felt that she couldn't hear anything or feel anything. Jacqueline slumped in the armchair and said, "This cannot be right, this cannot be true, there has been a mistake, I just saw my love this morning, he only had a cold, this isn't right Dylan, the tears wouldn't come, they just wouldn't come as Jacqueline had gone into some kind of trance, she felt she was having an out of body reaction and this wasn't really her. Colm tried to hug his mam but there was no reaction, he couldn't get any emotion out of her or movement, in essence, Jacqueline had become a statue.

Dylan put his hands on Jacqueline's face and said, "Listen Jacqueline, I am going to telephone the Doctor to come and see you and Fr Donnelly, then I am going to telephone Emily and Niamh". There was no response from Jacqueline, Dylan was getting concerned and promptly got in touch with Dr Clark to come immediately. Luckily, Dr Clark was available and was just about to go on his afternoon visits. The Doctor arrived 10 minutes later and gave Jacqueline a sedative and she was to stay in bed for the rest of the day.

Dylan couldn't reach Niamh at the University, so he had decided to drive there and see her personally, in the meantime, Emily had arrived home and was comforting Colm. Colm just kept repeating himself to Emily, "Dad had a cold, he had a headache, his headache has been there for weeks, why our Emily why! Why has he gone, it doesn't seem fair, it was just a cold, just a headache, it's not fair! Emily cuddled into Colm, and they cried it out. Emily too was struggling to take it all in, our dad gone, it doesn't make sense! Emily got up to make them a drink and called Aileen to come round as she was always good around Colm. "Oh! I must call Sara too, as mam will need our Auntie Sara, they were close.

Dylan arrived at the university and went to the main office to ascertain where Niamh was on campus, there was a bit of delay, protocol, data protection giving out personal information about a student, all the red tape, until Dylan lost his temper and went back to the car to get his driver's licence to verify his credentials. As Dylan walked across the campus Niamh was coming out of the Halsby building and looked across, "That looks like our Dylan? It cannot be, what is he doing here?". Niamh walked towards him, "Dylan she shouted". He turned around, "Niamh! "What is wrong Dylan! Is it mam, is it dad, what? Dylan grabbed Niamh tight, "It's your dad he has died this afternoon at the office, we have to wait for the cause of death for a few days". Niamh looked at Dylan, "Is this real, he cannot be? I just talked to him the other day he was joking around, and we just had that fantastic weekend, dad is fit he is fit! I want to see him, I want to see him now, take me to my dad! Dylan held her to calm her, "You cannot

161

not just yet pet, you cannot, I am sorry, let's go home, your mam has had the doctor and she he has given her a sedative". "Oh no! poor mam, yes, let's just go home quickly, I will let the office know". As Dylan and Niamh entered the office, Dylan apologised for this bad temper, the lady at the desk replied, "No need in the circumstances, really take care you two, sorry for your loss". Niamh hung on to Dylan until they got into the car. The numbness had set in, and Niamh was trying to hold herself together. Dylan drove as quick as he could but was wary of the speed limits along the main road.

Dylan stepped into the living room and Colm got out of the chair and moved towards Niamh they grasped each other with such pain and the tears flowed for an age. Dylan went straight upstairs to check on Jacqueline who was fast asleep. "Oh! My! dear sister-in-law", as he talked to himself. Dylan sat by the window ledge and stared into the ocean, "The sand and sea looked so ugly today, as if someone has ripped it all up". Dylan couldn't comprehend any of it, his loss hadn't set in at all, he was still on auto pilot.

Sara had arrived and joined her sister Aileen in the kitchen. Emily was trying to console Niamh and Colm. The kettle was boiling, and they all eventually sat around the kitchen table to talk about Jacqueline and how they could help her get through this. Dylan pointed out that we are all hurting, but we need to put Jacqueline first and do our best to get her through this and support each other along with the way. We all can help each other in our own way. Sara replied by saying, "I think you are right Dylan we need to stick together". I have put in for compassionate leave at the hospital so I can be here for the next 2 weeks 24/7 ". Aileen also contributed by saying, "Yes, I can be here to help out". Dylan got up and moved towards the telephone, "I must telephone Serena to let her know". "Haven't you told her yet Uncle Dylan", as Niamh looked at him with a rather surprised look on her face. "I haven't had the time really, I wanted to get you home from University". Niamh put her arms around Dylan and said, "You are such a great Uncle, you really are".

Dylan didn't get through to Serena, as she was with a client, and he left a message for her to call him at Jacquelines. Sara and Aileen did their best to get Niamh, Colm, and Emily to have a bite to eat, but was to no avail. Colm began to talk about his dad and how he felt he could have done more as he had noticed his dad taking painkillers quite regularly the past few weeks. Dylan reassured him that it wasn't his fault at all, no one is to blame. The day passed by, and the telephone rang at 6pm and it was Serena, she immediately put the telephone down and made her way to Jacquelines.

The sound of footsteps coming down the stairs as Jacqueline appeared, "What is everyone doing here, where is Declan?". Dylan grabbed her as she was unsteady on her feet, and helped her back to bed, reassuring that she needed to rest. Jacqueline looked far too tired to respond and fell back into a heavy sleep. Sara mentioned that we need to get the Doctor back tomorrow, I feel that Jacqueline is going to need some medical help, as the shock could have created temporary amnesia. Dylan agreed as did the rest of the family. Colm looked terribly worried about his mam, Niamh felt positive and said, "Mam will pull herself round I know she will".

Serena arrived and held Dylan like she had never held him before so tightly. Dylan began to get emotional and stopped himself from becoming too emotional, as he felt he had to be the strong one in the family.

Aileen began to make some sandwiches and insisted that each one of them would have to eat at least one sandwich, Aileen put her foot and down and demanded this was going to happen. They all looked up at Aileen with utter amazement they hadn't seen Aileen use that kind of manner, it was not usually her way, she was gentle and soft speaking. They all replied, "Yes, Aileen ok".

They all sat round the fire, reminiscing, talking, and talking about all the stories they could come up with that made them cheer up and it was working. They all had a smile on their face and the joy of talking about Jacqueline and Declan made it seem like it was in the present and not in the past. It was helping everyone to get through the night, as they talked and talked until the early hours. It was Serena who made the first move at 3am and suggested that Dylan stay with her that night and let Sara and Aileen stay Niamh, Colm, and Emily. "Sleep we all need to get some sleep". Sara slept in Jacqueline's room and Aileen took the settee. The lights went out at the Gibson household, it was a dark night. Tomorrow is another day....

Chapter 28

Jacqueline woke up in the early hours, she was not quite getting her bearings, her head was full of conflicting thoughts, one minute she is talking to Declan and the next minute she is screaming! Where is Declan. Her body was shattered with the loss and despair. Jacqueline began to surface, she still felt croggy from the effects of the sedative Dr Clark had given her, as she walked towards the bathroom, she began to wake up properly, as she looked into the mirror at herself, "Oh my what a state, I look awful". Jacqueline jumped into the bath to revive herself, as she always believed a good bath is a good way to refresh yourself. Jacqueline calmly lay there in the bath, and contemplated the events of yesterday, it was all coming back to her, and the floods of tears began to roll down her face. Jacqueline began to talk to herself, "I must get ahead of myself, I must pull myself together for the children, I must speak to Fr Donnelly today!"

Niamh and Emily knocked at the bathroom door, and Jacqueline assured them that she wouldn't be long. Niamh sighed with relief, "At least Mam is up and about, that's good isn't it our Emily". Emily put her arm around Niamh, "It is Niamh, we just have to get through this together".

Jacqueline came out of the bathroom and hugged her daughters tightly and explained that she needs to get to church right away. Niamh and Emily looked at one another and gasped! "Mam seems to be so spritely suddenly. Niamh understood this as she knew her mam would turn to the church for strength, as Niamh grabbed her mam's hand and gently spoke to her "It's ok mam Fr Donnelly is coming round this very hour to see you, no need to rush around mam, I called him earlier". Jacqueline stood back with a relieved smile on her face, "Oh, that's good, that's really good, I am so very glad he is coming, I will get dressed now". Jacqueline was on auto pilot functioning well in the circumstances. It was if she was just going through the motions, she felt like she was floating on air at this moment. Jacqueline turned to the Sacred Heart, which was mounted above the bed, Jacqueline began her conversation with God as she knelt by her bed with her Rosary Beads clasped around her hand she began to say, "I hope you will carry me through this Dear God, just like the Footprints in the Sand please do this for me". Jacqueline knelt whilst she went through the Rosary, it gave her so joy and strength, that feeling of enlightenment and peace, her stomach stopped churning for a moment.

Jacqueline heard the front door, it was Dylan, he had come to check on everyone, especially Colm, as he was worried about him and the effect it had on him seeing his dad like that. Colm was putting on a brave face, as he felt that he was the man of the house now, and it was his job to keep everyone going. Dylan was proud of Colm as they sat outside both staring at the calm sea and the grey clouds drifting along. The sand looks so passive and gloomy today, they continued chatting, changing the subject to football, "I hope the lads win this Saturday it would mean that they would be in the top 3 of the Champions league if they do, as Colm turned to Dylan". "Aye lad it should be a good un, we should go, your dad would want us to, he will be there in spirit he will". Colm felt guilty for feeling happy at the minute about the prospect of a great win. It was decided they would go.

Fr Donnelly arrived, and everyone joined Dylan and Colm in the garden, it was dismal morning, but no one cared, the clouds were beginning to lift and the sun was making its way through. Sara and Aileen had their thick duffle coats on and decided to have a good brisk walk along the beach; the beach was beautiful whatever the season. The sun began to shine gloriously, and seagulls were squawking their usual tunes, bantering away at each other. "I wonder what they are saying to each other", as Sara remarked on the continued squawking which was quite incessant this morning. "They do seem to be chattering away this morning don't they", as Aileen looked towards the Trow rocks where 7 of the seagulls were perched together. "It's a mystery nature, but it is a beautiful mystery. They walked in silence for some time, gathering their own thoughts, as they linked one another and squeezed each other's arm for comfort, no words were needed just that loving comfort was all that was needed.

Back at the Gibson's Fr Donnelly had put the kettle on and sat Jacqueline down at the kitchen table, he took over with his thoughtful manner. "Right Jacqueline, I will sort everything out for the funeral once we have heard from the mortuary, I will get Declan's body to the church so he can rest there, and then we will sort out the Vigil. Jacqueline just sat and agreed with everything, not really taking it in at this moment, just nodding away. Fr Donnelly was aware that he would have to carry Jacqueline through this. Fr Donnelly, prayed alongside Jacqueline and gave her the holy Sacrament, Jacqueline always felt that wonderful calmness and the sublime feeling receiving the Sacrament, recalling her poem she wrote a long time ago.

Twas the glow of the spirit gorging in the breast...
With childlike aspirations....
Calmness, peaceful remedies of flow-like rivers...
Stillness in body and soul....
Addressing the outside world, without blemish....
Sublime, perfection, unscathed....

Jacqueline felt at ease and wished that feeling would not subside and keep on going to keep her mind and body going during this awful, dreaded time in her life. Fr Donnelly wished her good health and left to get ready for morning Mass at the Church.

The telephone rang and the coroner explained to Jacqueline the outcome of Declan's death, it was a sudden aneurysm that had occurred, that was the cause of death. It seems that headaches he was having beforehand, and the trauma he received from the accident brought this about unfortunately. Jacqueline thanked the coroner and slowly put the telephone down as she walked into the kitchen she began to scream! Dylan and Colm ran into the kitchen, "Jacqueline! come on now! I have got you", as Dylan grabbed hold of her. "It was the coroner, the accident, and headaches, have killed him with an aneurysm, "Oh why did he have to be down the pit that day, why!". "I know it isn't fair, I know, come on nice cup of tea". Jacqueline sat down and calmed herself, as she looked at Colm, his pale worried face, "I am going make you your favourite breakfast son, you need it". Jacqueline prepared the bacon, eggs, fried bread with black pudding and two sausages, all Jacqueline wanted to think about was feeding her son and at that moment. Dylan helped her along and he also had a good breakfast, making sure Jacqueline ate at least some bacon and toast. Colm didn't disappoint his mam and ate it even though he didn't really want it.

Later that day they all gathered around to talk about the vigil and the funeral arrangements. Love Divine or Love's excelling was Declan's favourite, although he didn't go to church that much, he was a believer and prayed in his own time, he felt going to church Easter and Christmas was his way of giving back to his faith. The Vigil was for close friends and family, Dylan went through the list to spare Jacqueline anymore heartache, as he felt the more they did for Jacqueline, the smoother the process, Dylan was very grateful to Fr Donnelly who went all out to sort the services and the funeral buffet which would be held in the Community Centre, as there were so many who wanted to contribute, Declan was a popular man at the local pit and also at the shipyard. Everything was set for the Vigil and the funeral.

Niamh had gained compassionate leave from university, and she had no intentions on going back until after funeral, her thoughts were far away from university, as she tried to grasp all the different emotions she was feeling, Niamh, felt comfort from being with her dear sister Emily, who was a great strength to her. Sara felt so helpless, all she could do was to be there for Jacqueline her dear sister, "I must get Jacqueline out and about after the funeral", as she thought to herself that would be the best thing for her not to dwell too much. Time is the only cure for such grief, for time is a great healer, but using that time to deflect from grief isn't a bad idea, Sara was setting out a plan of her own for Jacqueline.

Serena had arrived in readiness for the Vigil, it was Dylan she was more concerned about as he hadn't shown much emotion since the death of his brother, Dylan just didn't stand still enough to grasp the effect of grief, his way was to keep Colm going, but Colm was doing much better than he had imagined. Serena was ready for the fall with Dylan, hoping it would come sooner rather than later, as she felt the effects of later may hit even harder, for how can anyone put grief into a category, its essence is a soul-searching factor of each individual as they come to terms with their own grief. Serena was ready to embrace Dylan with all her heart and support him. Serena hadn't experienced such grief in her family, and wasn't sure how to approach it, only to just be sympathetic and supportive, it was hard one to call, as Serena was feeling isolated at this time as she hadn't really had a good conversation with Dylan since the death of his brother. She felt the only strategy would be to let Dylan approach her with his feelings and not keep asking him if he is ok, as she felt his tone the last time, so cool and distant. "I need to give Dylan his space too, as she thought out loud, what to do for the best, take it minute by minute".

They were all ready for the Vigil, just a very few close friends for this service as the Church would be packed solid for the funeral the next day. The Vigil was beautiful Fr Donnelly so caring, and his words of wisdom always appreciated by many.

The night seemed to last forever, everyone was clock watching all night, sombre as the soft sea was the Gibson household that night. Jacqueline felt that her legs would give way on the morning of the funeral, she gave herself a good talking too and her prayers were answered that morning, her legs floated down the isle of the church and her body seem to have a will of his own. Everyone gave they condolences, those echoed voices of good wishes seem to echo on and on his Jacqueline's mind.

The beautiful service was over, and everyone gathered in the community centre, so much food, it looked like everyone in the village had cooked. Jacqueline and the family were overwhelmed with such support, kindness, not to mention generosity.

Jacqueline agreed to put on some of Declan's favourite songs, he loved blues and jazz, and his close friends played the piano, cello and saxophone. For a moment Jacqueline could see Declan's face next to her, it was fleeting moment but none the less, it made Jacqueline smile for she truly felt he was next to her.

Dylan was not paying much attention to Serena, as he was in full conversation with Declan's friends who were also Dylan's friends too. Serena stood back in the hall, Fr Donnelly caught her eye as he walked towards and took a glass of wine over to her., he felt that she may need it. "Come take a seat Serena, how are you my dear". Serena looked a little tearful, "I am not sure how I am Fr Donnelly, Dylan is so evasive". "Give it time my dear, he will let you in when he is ready to let you in, just be patient my dear". Serena took a sip of her wine and said, "Yes, you are probably right Fr, this is so kind of you to come and talk to me". If you ever need to chat my dear, you know where I am. Serena couldn't believe it a priest talking to me, I am not a Catholic, he knows that but still he gives out his words of encouragement and kindness. Maybe I should convert, she thought in her mind.

Serena made her way over to Jacqueline, "Come sit by me awhile", as Jacqueline got up to greet Serena with a loving hug and kissed her on the cheek. Serena was lost for words, she expressed her deep condolences to Jacqueline, "I cannot imagine how you feel, as I have never experienced such a loss, but if you ever need to cry on someone's shoulder mine is always ready for you". Serena couldn't think of anything else to say. Jacqueline responded by saying, "You are here pet, and more importantly you are here for Dylan, don't think I haven't noticed that he looks as if he is avoiding you. Let him do it his way, he loves you so much and I feel that he is frightened to crumble in front of you, that's just my view in knowing him so well". "That makes sense to me Jacqueline, I will bear that in mind".

The evening went off well, and everyone said their goodbyes, Dylan came over to Jacqueline and Serena, "Let me see you ladies' home". Jacqueline replied, "I am walking along the beach with our Sara Dylan, you see to Serena". Serena didn't want to go home; she would rather stay at Dylans. Dylan put his arm around Serena and welcomed her suggestion that she stay at his. As they arrived at Dylans flat, he got out the wine and whiskey, they sat up drinking, Serena didn't stop him drinking as she knew it would all come to the surface once the whiskey had hit him, and she was right; she held him all night as he grieved his heart out. The day had ended, and the morning was a new dawn, a new day….

Chapter 29

The sun was shining through the curtains in Niamh's room as she turned over in bed to take a glimpse of the shimmering sun peeking out at the side of the curtain. Niamh sauntered towards the window and looked out at the clear blue sky; the surfers were eagerly lined up for their daily ride on the waves. The image of the surfers gliding on the waves, how free and easy they look, why cannot life be that way, as Niamh stood for a while alone with her own thoughts and feelings; a sense of serenity came upon Niamh as she watched the surfers smoothly gliding away.

Colm knocked briskly on Niamh's bedroom door, which made Niamh jump out of her skin as she was far away in her serene thoughts of peace. Colm had brought her back to reality with a ban… "You up our Niamh", as he shouted, "I am awake now brother" as she turned to him. "I didn't get you up". You are already dressed, what you are talking about", as he candidly smirked at Niamh. Niamh smiled at him, she had forgotten that cheeky smirk, she had missed it at university. "We are ok, aren't we?", as Colm tried to convince himself that everything was going to be ok and he wanted Niamh to be ok, as he knew how close Niamh was to her dad. We all had Dad's affection, but Niamh always seem to make dad shine with her book learning and her wit, they seemed to comply with one another with their eagerness for knowledge. Dad was the historian and mathematician, and Niamh was always delving into the literary world of period drama and the history of it, they both seem to come together with their findings, they talked a lot. It was going to be harder for Niamh. Colm felt that getting his mam back on track with the outside world would be much better for all of them and it could benefit Niamh too, after all, Niamh and her mam were both literary buddies. It was if Colm began to grow up in that moment and was talking to himself more like a man rather than a boy. Colm felt like his dad was looking down on him and saying, "You are the man of the house lad, so get on with it". It was an extraordinary feeling he felt, but a warm feeling inside of him that was urging him on.

Emily was talking on the telephone with Belinda, and it was decided that Belinda would open the shop and Emily would leave her in charge for the morning. Aileen entered the room and sat with Emily, "You see to the shop pet, and I will see to your mam, don't worry, keep yourself busy pet". Emily wanted to spend the morning with Niamh before she headed back to university. "I have left Belinda in charge this morning Aunt Aileen, I will go in after lunch, is that ok with you Auntie Aileen", "Of course it is pet, you have a nice time with Niamh".

Emily and Niamh walked all the way along the Beach until they got to the promenade, their special place when they were younger. "Aw there our Niamh, there is our favourite fountain, remember when we used to come in and splash about and get told off", they both laughed and laughed. The Fountain had been renovated since then and it had a beautiful sculpture of an eagle as a set piece which was illuminated. They both sat alongside it and embraced their happy times along the promenade and the buzz of life and happiness embroiled their inner being at that moment, they were intertwining like two peas in a pod. As Niamh turned to Emily she began to say, "I wish I wasn't going back to university, I don't feel that energy I had". "Oh, Our Niamh don't be silly, you will get that energy back, you will, I know you, you are strong, just think of our dad, he would be so disappointed if you gave it up, he would you know". Niamh began to cry, "I know, I know, he would, he would, Oh! You always say the right things our Emily, love you for that". They hugged and briskly walked along the promenade, it was getting so chilly, as Christmas was just around the corner. "Oh! look Saveloys, let's stop and have one, OH! A hot cinnamon drink let's do that". They were all warmed up and felt that warm bond, that strong bond, that would get them through anything.

Jacqueline, Aileen, and Sara were getting ready to go shopping, food shopping. Sara had persuaded Jacqueline to come with them. Sara knew how to coax her, as she knew Jacqueline wouldn't leave her in charge of buying flour, eggs, and other ingredients to make up Yorkshire puddings, and apple pies. Sara always bought the wrong flour, wrong eggs, and hadn't got a clue on what to pick when deciding which spices to buy with which apples. Sara's plan to get Jacqueline out of the house was working. "Good job Sara", as Aileen winked at her.

They went into the Newcastle Town Centre, the Christmas window displays were outstanding, the festive season was upon us, it was going to be a tough one to say the least for the Gibson family. Jacqueline heart sunk as she walked past Mackies; Mackies! it was Declan and Jacqueline's special shop for Christmas, they had it all. Sara and Aileen steered Jacqueline towards Lisles haberdashery store it has recently been refurbished and they hadn't disappointed there was lots of goodies, from Christmas ornaments to a great selection of books at the bottom of the shop. Jacqueline was taken with this new look and moved quickly towards the books; they had some great new cookery books as well has some great novels to read. Having spent over an hour in the shop, they all came out with great gifts for Christmas. The mood had lightened, and it was a great distraction, Lisles is on our favourite list from now on, as the three them linked one and other. Jacqueline was the first to mention that it was time to do the food shopping. Sara had other ideas she wanted Jacqueline to have a further distraction, they all went to the cinema to watch a movie, "The Railway Children". Sara, Jacqueline, and Aileen left the cinema in good spirits, the day was surreal, it didn't feel like they had suffered a bereavement, it was the escapism that was saving them from feeling that sense of loss. Sara knew that escapism was the best remedy for them all today, and she was determined to relive escapism on a regular basis with Jacqueline so as not to let her dwell too much.

As they all arrived home all their packages and food parcels, it was time to get the kettle on and the tea started. Jacqueline prepared the evening meal; she was happy to be distracted and very thankful to her lovely sisters. The long night will come soon enough as she kept her thoughts to herself, almost like wearing a veil on your face to hide the pain.

They all sat around the table and Jacqueline spoke to Colm and asked about Bernadette, Colm was happy to talk about the football session coming up, rather than get into a conversation about Bernadette. Aileen pointed out that she had telephoned this morning and was hoping Colm would return her call. Jacqueline responded by saying, "It would be rude Colm not to call her back, you have not been brought up to be rude my son". Colm sighed a little, and replied with a "Yes, mam, will do, later". Niamh was quiet at the table; she was contemplating her return to university. Sara asked when the semester breaks for Christmas. Niamh looked up rather dismayed, "7 days' time, I have exams next week". "You will be fine Niamh, you know your stuff", as Sara glanced at Niamh with pride, "Go girl, no fear". Jacqueline went over to Niamh and whispered, "Don't forget what you have learned and what you have become; your hard work will pay off, keep focused pet", Jacqueline kissed her daughter on the forehead.

The evening passed by so quickly, Jacqueline almost dreaded going to bed, but this evening she was so exhausted with the shopping trip and cooking, she fell into her bed without a thought in her head. That wasn't the case at Dylan's flat he was slowly recovering from his binge drinking. He had never binged so much in his life, and he didn't like it at all. Serena cleaned his flat, it was mess; a good cooked a meal was on the menu; she needed the practice she felt, as the wedding wasn't that far away… so much to do. Dylan was not focused on anything, and the wedding was not on his mind at all. Serena knew in her heart she would have to get Dylan through this heartbreaking time, the biggest problem she faces is the best man, as Declan was to be the best man, that would have to be up to Dylan. Serena had decided to put the conversation on wedding plans on the back burner until Christmas and the New Year was over. Serena would alert her mum and dad, as Serena wanted a quiet Christmas and she planned to have that with Dylan. It was time for Serena to have that talk with her mum and dad about Christmas.

Arriving home Serena greeted her mum and dad at the door as she hugged her mum and dad tightly, "Oh that was a hug with meaning ", as Charlotte looked straight into her daughter's eyes, knowing that there was something behind that squeezing hug. "Let's all go into the Study", as Serena moved swiftly towards the study door. Serena began to quickly get to the point, "I am going to spend Christmas Day with Dylan and his family, he needs me there with his family, especially this year, I know you will understand. Mr Inskip was not impressed that Serena did not want to spend Christmas day with them, Mrs Inskip on the other hand sympathised with Serena as she knew that Dylan would need his own family on Christmas and Serena needed to be there as she would be his family soon. "Boxing Day dad, we will spend Boxing Day with you, just this once dad please don't make a fuss about this". Mr Inskip looked into Serena's eyes and realised that he was losing his daughter in some way, but he couldn't be prouder of her compassion and commitment to her future husband. He hugged her with conviction.

Dylan at this time was getting to grips with the loss of his brother, he went out on a run to clear his head, as he ran all the way to the Beach across the promenade and out to the lighthouse. He hadn't realised he had been running for an hour as he sat on a bedded rock, getting his breath back, he sat with this thoughts and memories and cradled himself with the sheer pain he was feeling, and thought about what Declan once said to him when he was teenager, "Life is set to try you and try you at its peril, be ready lad for the ups and downs and life and don't not falter, just pick yourself up and dust yourself off". Dylan at that moment felt a strong presence of his brother, as the wind wisped by his shoulder. He realised he wasn't too far away from Declan's cottage, and slowly walked toward the back door to see how everyone was getting on.

Sara opened the back door, the family were all seated in the living room, apart from Colm who was on the telephone to Bernadette. Jacqueline got up to greet Dylan, "We have just said our Goodbye's to Niamh, Aileen has kindly driven her back to university". "Oh no! I have missed her; I would have taken her back you know". It's fine Dylan, you sit yourself down, cup of tea?". Yes, please, need one after this lengthy run I have just had. "You got rid of the cobwebs then", as Jacqueline smiled at Dylan. "Oh yes our Jacques, I have".

The conversation turned to Christmas and how they would celebrate with some joy, as they all agreed Declan would not want them to sit miserable at the Christmas table, the talk evaporated into all the Christmas's they had in the past, which were so memorable. Declan was always the first to get the party started, LP's 45's on the go Blues and Jazz, Four Tops Beatle, Elvis, Old blue eyes, they will celebrate it as if he was there in spirit. A warm glow came over of the family. Colm walked into the room and greeted Dylan, he was happy his uncle had turned up, he wanted so to talk to him about Bernadette.

Dylan and Colm went into the kitchen and Colm began to tell Dylan how Bernadette was so caring and thoughtful towards him, and he was starting to like Bernadette a lot, but he wondered if his emotions were spilling over because of losing his dad. Dylan calmed Colm down, as he was getting a little frantic, his emotions were running high. "You should embrace these feelings Colm and enjoy all the attention, don't over think lad, just enjoy your first journey of having strong feelings for a girl, don't doubt it just go with the flow". Colm looked up at Dylan and gave him a sly smirk raising his eyebrow, "Ok Uncle, you are the expert, I will be on your back, if things go pear shaped". Dylan shrugged his head back, "Trust me, stick with me kid, I will learn the ropes". Dylan patted Colm on the back. Colm was feeling a little more relaxed now. They both went back into the living room and joined the rest of family as they enjoyed their night of togetherness in readiness for the big event Christmas Day...

Chapter 30

Niamh jumped up in her bed, it was early, it was exam day! as she lay there staring at the ceiling, going through all the pointers her Tutor had outlined in the lecture, she was so methodical, and was sticking to her strategy, as she put on the radio, the room in her dormitory looked so small, it always seemed to be every time she returned from her home, as the cottage was so spacious. She smiled to herself and put the radio on it was playing, "Everlasting Love", by the Love Affair, she began to sing along; Niamh began to stare at her photograph of her mam and dad and shouted out, "You are here dad I know you are you will always be here for me, I know that ". As she strolled to the bathroom; a bath to refresh all those nerves flying about, "I am ready as she lay in the bath, I am ready for this one; the exam is literature, it's the Romantic movement, I know it by heart". Her head went under water, Niamh gasped, jumped out of the bath, and quickly got herself tidied, hair done, sweater and slacks on.

The exam was a success, all the questions were everything Niamh had revised, they were there for the taking, the only doubt she had was she had overwritten too much, her paper was lengthy, but more is best she felt, few is missing the point. Niamh's thoughts turn to home, her feelings were strong to get home, to feel that warmth of the big coal fire, sitting around the hearth with her big sister.

Jacqueline was looking forward to having all her children at home for Christmas, as they were her whole life now, she relished that comfort, for they were her crutch that would see her through her heartache, as she sauntered through the Christmas decorations, she had an idea, why not Colm and Dylan do the Tree this Eve of Christmas.

Christmas Eve became the Eve of something so strange in the Gibson household, an aura of change seemed to spread around the room, as they all gathered, Dylan, Serena, Aileen, Arthur,

Sara, John had arrived, and the festivities had begun. The whole evening seemed to evolve around Dylan and Serena and their forthcoming wedding, as Serena steered Jacqueline away into the kitchen, "Jacqueline I wanted to ask you about being a Catholic Convert", Jacqueline couldn't believe it, she was so happy that Dylan and Serena were going to have a Catholic wedding. Jacqueline explained to Serena what would happen, she would have to be baptised. Firstly, we need to call on Fr Donnelly, a good time to approach him would be after mid-night mass. They both sat around the kitchen table, "how is your mam and dad about this sudden change Serena?", Serena quivered a little, "I haven't told them yet". "Oh, best do that soon then". "I will Boxing Day, I know it will be a big shock, but it's our Wedding, I will make them see that, mum will be fine, dad, he will be shocked, but he will get over it in time". "Oooh Serena, are you sure, it's a big step". "I know, but it's that step that I feel so strongly about, and it won't leave me". Dylan entered the room, "Come on you two, charades, let's get started ". The evening went by so quickly and Fr Donnelly was more than happy to accommodate Serena. The Journey in Faith for Serena would begin in the New Year in readiness for the big day on 11 April...

At the Inskips, Boxing Day was a tense affair, as Mr Inskip was finding it hard to come to terms with, Serena converting to a Catholic, what has happened to my special girl, as he sauntered around the room with a pensive look on his face. Mrs Inskip would be the instigator to turn things around, as Charlotte had a unique way of changing her husband's mind. "Jonathan, remember when Serena was young, 9-year-old, when she shocked you, she rode her pony and bent down to you and said, "Daddy don't look so shocked daddy, I am growing up and I can handle anything daddy". Remember, you were so amazed. Afterall being a Catholic isn't so bad, it's not the end of the world, Serena will still be our precious daughter no matter what. Jonathan suddenly became so emotional but understood where his wife was going with this. The day ended on a high note, and all was restored at the Inskip household.

The New Year passed by like a flash of lightening, Colm was at ease with Bernadette now, they decided they would be friends, as Bernadette was pursuing her art at college. Colm felt she was a great friend during the past months, and he felt comfortable with that. Niamh had passed her exams with flying colours, and Emily and Frankie's romance was blossoming. Jacqueline liked Frankie a lot, he had been a rock for Emily during the bereavement. The Christmas and New Year period had certainly brought everyone together, and Jacqueline was so happy with the numerous distractions, her heart was heavy, and she was grateful that Fr Donnelly was there to lend a hand.

Fr Donnelly had prepared the 7-week session with Serena, it was elevating Serena to the point that she felt this connecting door that made her feel complete, she couldn't understand it, but she was so eager to keep on learning about her new faith. It was important to Serena that she be completely ready for the Wedding Ceremony as it was quite a lengthy ordeal.

As the weeks went past Serena began to engage with Catholic Mass and was becoming very fond of Our Lady, the Virgin Mary as she was central to the Catholic faith. The Hail Mary prayer became constant in Serena's mind. Dylan was conscious of how his future wife was developing, in his mind Serena was pulling out all the stops, and he had never imagined that he could love someone as much as he loved Serena, for Serena had become his saviour, his North, South, East, and West.

Dylan was grabbling with the thought that Declan wouldn't be there to be his best man and the only one that can take his place is our Colm. Let's see if he is up for this big occasion, let's hope so. Colm was busy in the office finishing off the dimensions given to him for the ship that was in Dry Dock, the Linesman, he was becoming a good draughtsman. It was almost lunch time and as he walked over to the canteen he bumped into Dylan, and they had lunch together. "I have question for you lad, it's a big ask, but would you be my Best Man". Colm almost fell off his chair, "Me! wow! I would be honoured to be your Best Man our Dylan". "Phew! That's a big weight off my mind! We need to be

180

suited and booted lad, first fitting next weekend". "What do you mean, what are we wearing?", as Colm looked bemused. "Listen and learn lad for the future; we need to be fitted for our morning suits top hat and tails lad, with gloves; the classic look". "Gawd! our Dylan that's a bit over the top, isn't it?". "You won't think so when you have been fitted trust me, you will look the part ". "If you say so our Dylan", as Colm rolled his eyes with an unimpressed look upon his face.

Meanwhile, Serena was multi-tasking, fitting in her Journey of Faith, with her busy daily schedule at work, and sorting out the bridesmaids, which would be Niamh, Emily, and Serena's Maid of Honour her best friend, Trudy. The Bridesmaids dresses were already in the shop ready for their first fitting. Serena had a turnabout in relation to who was making the Wedding Cake, she felt that Jacqueline would be the best candidate and it would keep her occupied. Jacqueline was happy to accommodate, in fact, she was elated. It was to be a three-layer sponge cake, chocolate inside with a gorgeous vanilla icing with pink and white rosebuds. The Bride's Bouquet would be pink and white roses. Serena had left the cars to be sorted out with her father, who seemed to be taking everything in his stride. Charlotte oversaw making sure the flowers were made up in the correct way.

The day had arrived for Serena to be fitted with her wedding dress, it was white satin with a pale shimmering light pink underskirt, the embroidery was hand stitched with elegant beading with shimmers of white and light pink beads; the dress had a long trail and a high neck of elegant lace. As Serena stepped into her dress her mum Charlotte was overwhelmed with emotion; "You look absolutely stunning my pet, the dress is so graceful my pet, the tiara is so detailed with tiny beads to compliment the dress, you look sensational, as Charlotte wiped the tears from her cheek. "Mum don't cry, you make me cry and my mascara will run all of the place". The Designer stood back in the shop and said, "This is my best ever, thank you, you look beautiful" They all sat down and had a glass of bubbly on the house to celebrate.

Niamh, Emily, Trudy had entered the shop, "Oh! I see! We missed the bubbly then have we", as Trudy winked at Serena. "You can have yours, don't worry after you have been fitted, ok", as Serena winked at Trudy. The Girls looks fabulous in their shimmering light dusty pink bridesmaid dresses, a great accompaniment to Serena's dress. "Let the party begin", as Trudy raised a glass to Serena. Niamh and Emily were feeling a little strange in their long dresses, as they hadn't worn a long dress before, it was always midi or mini dresses for them. "It's only for the day our Emily, "W do look rather fetching in them, don't you think". Emily giggled out loud, "Ooh if you say so Sis", as Emily bowed gracefully towards Niamh as if she was bowing to Royalty.

Dylan, Colm, and Serena's father were on their way to the shop to get their morning suits fitted. Colm was a little apprehensive but soon got into the mood. Serena's father was delighted to wear a morning suit, he looked rather fetching. Dylan looked suave his morning suit and Colm was so surprised. "I look rather dashing in my suit, don't I". "You certainly do our Colm". As Mr Inskip looked on at the two of them and thought to himself, "Dylan is a good man, I am giving my daughter to a good man", as he gave Dylan a thoughtful look and smiled, "You will do nicely Dylan". Dylan smiled back, "That's good future father-in-law". They too celebrated with a glass of bubbly, it was Colm's first taste of the bubbly stuff, all the bubbles went up his nose, he quite liked though, as Dylan winked at him.

Everything was all set and ready for the big day, it looked a rather brisk and sunny day as Serena drew her curtains and opened her window to breath that lovely fresh air, she was light footed as she went into her bathroom, the butterflies hadn't appeared at all, Serena was all of glow and dizzy with excitement.

Dylan Stayed at the Gibson household, as it was decided, as is customary for the Groom to stay alongside the Best Man. They were all up with the lark, anticipating the great day, Dylan was feeling a wee bit nervous, he wanted everything just right. Colm was as calm as a cucumber, he never got ruffled our laid-back Colm. His demure was starting to rub off on Dylan. They both looked dapper in their outfits, Jacqueline was taken back with the two dashing young men in her living room, as she was careful to hold her emotions in, as she had already given herself a talking to earlier that morning.

The car had arrived, a Rolls Royce was outside ready to go, Jacqueline would wait on Mrs Inskip to arrive in her Rolls Royce, it was fitting for Jacqueline to travel with Serena's mum The three bridesmaids were on their way to the Church who were staying at Trudy's, they decided to have a bonding session the night before the wedding.

Serena was ready, as she came down the stairs to greet her father, he took her hand and said, "You are amazing, you look so beautiful". "You don't look so bad yourself dad, rather dapper". As she linked her father, and he helped her into the car and carried a trail so well.

Fr Donnelly was all set to go, dressed in his wedding attire, a cream chasuble and liturgical stole and white cassock, he greeted Dylan with a firm handshake and warm smile. The cars were starting to arrive and Bernice from the choir was ready to sing Ave Maria, as Serena and her father walked down the aisle, the music resonated around the room, Bernice was accompanied by David on the Cello and Simon on the piano, Ian played the violin; a moment of spiritual excellence evolved in every space of the church. Although the service was lengthy, but there was no doubt, the contents sealed will stay forever in our hearts. As they walked out of the church Bernice finished with a beautiful song, "Because you come to me". It took Jacqueline's breath away as that song, our song, "Our song, mine and Declan's", as she whispered to herself. She felt like her heart would never beat again.

They all made their way to the reception, Colm was mulling over his Best Man speech, "I am just going to get straight to the point, Dylan is a great guy, great Uncle, great Mentor, and great human being. A rock that stood by us all in our hour of need. On a lighter note, Dylan is a prankster, watch out Serena, he will catch you by surprise, he is always playing jokes on me. He sent me down the post office once to pick up a parcel, he said it was an oral parcel, the postmaster said, "That's a joke lad no such thing as an oral parcel". The room filled with laughter. It turned out to be an emotional speech, but nevertheless it was a worthy speech.

Jacqueline took herself off to the side of the lake a quiet spot to contemplate her place in life now Declan has gone, "Where am I to be God", she asked as she looked up to the sky. She got a glimpse of the sea in the background; A poem suddenly appeared in her mind out of nowhere.

The Sea:
A Wilderness of life...
Full of Strife...
A singing Nightingale
So fragile so vain...
It's capture, its agony, its pain...

Life has left me stranded...
Like a caged bird....
Waiting and wondering
That sound, that moment to be heard...
A journey to be told....
Sequences to unfold...

As Jacqueline gazed across at the sea, a change was occurring within her, but she had no idea what was in store for her future. New beginnings......

THE END...

Milton Keynes UK
Ingram Content Group UK Ltd.
UKHW010459080224
437425UK00015B/352